A Farthin

Margaret Cooper Evans is a historical writer and re-enactor. A living history interpreter and a speaker on the lives of women in the 17th Century. She joined The Sealed Knot re-enactment society in 1996. Since then she has played the part of a Baggage Woman, a Musketeer, Goodwyfe, a Lady, and a Farmers Wife on the Living History camp. Her research culminated in her first factual History book; The Women of the English Civil War published in 2015. She makes 17th Century clothing and cooks authentic 17th Century food. Margaret has had articles published in the mainstream British press and specialist historical magazines. She lives in Oxfordshire with her husband and two cats.

Also by this author

Factual History

The Women of the English Civil War

Historical Fiction

1955

Modern Fiction

Jago

Hillary Long Mysteries

Upsidedown in Overdown
Summertime in Overdown
Christmas in Overdown
Man Down in Overdown
Halloween in Overdown; Part 1
Murder at Overdown Manor: Halloween Part 2
Evil in Overdown
Heart of Overdown

MARGARET COOPER EVANS

A FARTHING FOR OXFORDE

The story of one woman's life during the

English Civil War

First Published by Nuova Stella Publishing
2018

Covers by Andrew Evans
ISBN: 0-9934068-3-1
ISBN-13: 978-0-9934068-3-6

With thanks to
Andrew Evans for his support, proof reading and book cover design.

Nuova Stella Publishing

Contents

Oxfordshire

Map of Oxford 1643

Looking down from the North.
South Oxford is at the top of the page.

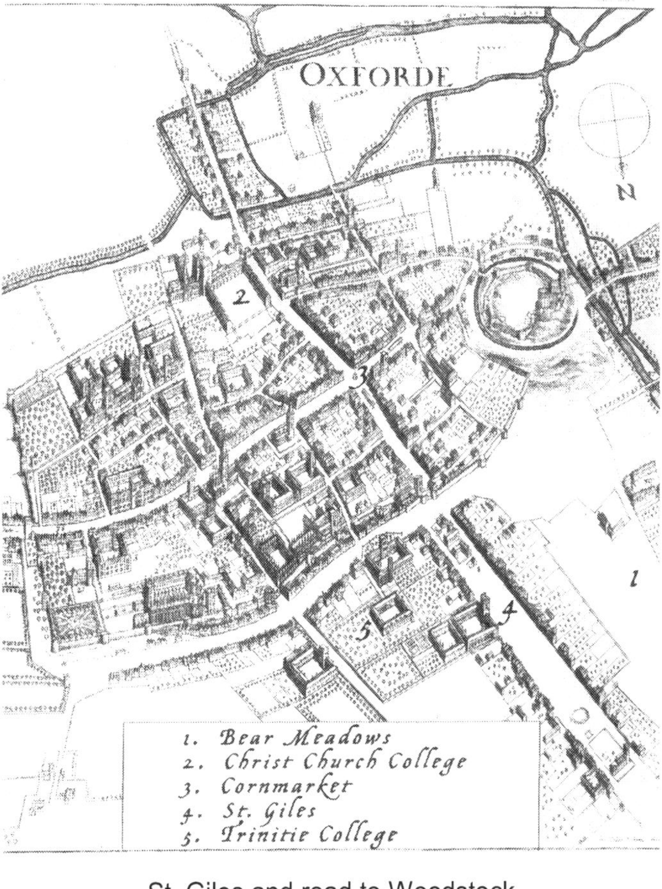

St. Giles and road to Woodstock
is at the bottom of this page

Introduction

Oxford 1609

I am waiting in the Cornmarket, newly arrived, dusty and dirty from the Hertfordshire post coach. My name is Anne Farthing, I think I am on the edge of Castle Street in Oxford. I don't know the city at all, so I couldn't tell you for sure. I'm sitting on my boxes waiting to start my new life with my aunt Susannah and uncle Thomas. I am told they live just outside the Oxford City walls in a cottage on Bear Meadow.

Mother is punishing me. Estranging me from my family and my home. She doesn't realise that it will be a relief for me to be away from her. I don't think she will beat my brother as much as she did me. She loves him. She scolds him, but that is all. Perhaps she will beat him, now I am gone.

I am to be apprenticed to my aunt, Susannah, to learn the trade of a midwife. Always needed, so I will be never out of work, so I am told. I fidget, scratching the flea bites around my ankles, watching the crowds pass by.

Unfamiliar strangers. A new life, a new place. Away from mother, I will have some freedom, I can't wait to see where it will lead me.

I close my eyes and think back to the day this all started.

Theobalds Palace, Hertfordshire,

August 1609

"Anne! Anne!" I could hear mother's anxious voice calling for me through the hedges of the lush green maze. I stifled a giggle as I sat with Henry, we had been holding hands and kissing on the cold stone seat under the laurel bush.

"Oh for God's sake where are you hiding child?" She sounded frustrated. "Anne?"

I heard her footsteps on the gravel getting closer, and the swish of her dark blue silk dress against the greenery. Henry put his hand over my mouth which excited me so I pulled closer to him.

"J' taime." I whispered watching his handsome face. He was taller than me at sixteen, his fairish hair tousled and made a brighter yellow by the summer sun.

"Of course you do," he whispered softly against my cheek, his newly growing beard soft on my skin, "I am, after all, your Prince." I smiled up at him and he kissed me passionately in the new French style.

Mother was suddenly upon us and pulled us apart. Her hands were bony and strong, she really hurt both of our arms. We squealed and struggled like stuck pigs.

When she saw my lover she fell into a deep curtsey. "My Lord, I beg your pardon." Her eyes narrowed spitefully at me. Princes did not get the blame for anything. I knew it would be my fault. With Mother, everything was always my fault.

"God's teeth, Mother it's 1609." I spat at her before the scolding could start.

My mother Katherine was a tall, handsome, neat and tidy woman. Thin, wiry and very strong. She and father had been brought from their home in Scotland to teach the Royal children of King James and Queen Anne, after whom I had been named.

"I know the date." She barked in her Scots burr as she shook me. "Have you been despoiled?"

"What?" I didn't know what she meant.

"Not by me." Prince Henry smiled. "Not yet anyway." He winked cheekily at me and gave a short sarcastic bow to my Mother as he swaggered off. The gold braid of his velvet burgundy jacket glinted in the late afternoon sun. "Shall I send William to you madam?" He asked, as he walked through the warm shadows of the maze, not bothering to turn around.

"To be sure." Mother pulled herself upright, her neatly curled glossy brown hair bobbed in an errant playful breeze, her face flushed scarlet.

As soon as Henry was out of sight, she pulled me by the arm out of the greenery of the maze and along the gravel pathway to our wing of the great red brick house. My feet were hardly touching the ground. She was still so angry with me that she was shaking. We got through the arched stone door where she pushed me violently onto the cold slab floor of the kitchen. I tried to get up, but she put her well-heeled shoe in the small of my back.

Soon a plain faced, brown haired young man about the same age as Prince Henry came through the door from the dining room.

He looked scared. "You called for me madam?" I looked up at him and smiled, he looked confused.

Mother's heel dug a little deeper. "Damn you. You just can't stop, can you?" she swore at me. "On the floor William, smartly now."

As we lay side by side. I could see the fire had been made up ready for the cooking of the evening meal to commence. Logs had been laid over tinder, flints and stones stood ready to be sparked.

I looked across at William who had closed his eyes tightly. Just as well, there was a dead mouse by the table leg just in front of his face.

I could hear the maidservants and the cooks chatter, coming into the kitchen, ready to start work.

"Madam." Meggie the old housekeeper started to speak. "This is not the place, we need to start the dinner."

Mother's ferocious stare was enough to silence her on the spot. She picked up a carpet beater and spanked me and William in turn with it. William was Henry's whipping boy. No one was allowed to lay a finger on a future King, so William took the punishment for his master. Being used to this kind of treatment, he had carefully padded his breeches with small feather pillows. As the whip and crack of the carpet beater hit his well-padded buttocks he let out mock cries of agony. I could hardly feel the willow on my skin as I wore a shift, an underskirt, and a bum roll, under my linen lined dress.

Unfortunately for me, I kept smiling as the swish and blat of the carpet beater did not reach any part of me that hurt. Mother noticed.

"William," she snapped, "you have taken the Prince's punishment like a man. You may go."

"Anne, pick up your skirts." She pulled me to face her. "Now."

It wasn't long before my humiliation was complete and the willow carpet beater cut through my white linen shift and blood began to show against the white cloth. I could hear the staff mumbling as a hand caught my mother's arm mid swipe, a voice I knew well shouted.

"Enough!"

My father, Thomas, pulled me from the floor.

"Wife, take thee some good beer and cake, calm thy temper and come to me. I shall take this creature to her chamber."

I will not feel pain, I will not feel pain. I told myself again and again, biting the side of my hand, as I climbed the cold stone stairs to my room. My father kept pushing me in my back. Every step stung, I could feel the warmth of the blood bursting from the splits in my skin. In my chamber, my father looked at me with what I can only describe as disgust.

I couldn't sit down.

"Are you still a maid?" He asked, his face flushed with embarrassment. He walked to the stone mullioned window that overlooked the well-kept kitchen garden to look out. His handsome face unable to look at my reddened, tear stained one.

It was now getting towards late afternoon and the ruby sun was dropping behind the trees.

"Yes, father." It was obvious to him I didn't know what he meant.

"Has the Prince put his dogge in your manger?" He didn't look at me but I could see he coloured scarlet from the neck up.

I did know what that meant. The maids constantly spoke of their men and compared their dogges, size, girth, satisfaction, so I had a very good idea.

"No." I blurted out, tears burning my eyes. "It was just a buss. He loves me."

Father spun on his heel. "Anne Farthing you are a simple child, a kiss leads to other intimacies. You cannot allow the Prince to practice on you, as for love, the Prince loves all his subjects. It is his job."

"I'm nearly sixteen, old enough to marry," I snapped at him. Immediately realising I had made a mistake. I stared at father as he turned round. His long brown hair lay in luxuriant curls on his starched white Belgian lace collar. He wore the burgundy sash across his black doublet that distinguished him as the teacher of the King's children. He was an imposing looking man, tall like my mother, but with kind eyes, unlike my mother.

"Princes do not marry commoners Anne. He cannot and would not marry you." He frowned at me. "I think you had better stay with your aunt in Oxfordshire for a while, out of harms' way."

"Excuse me sir." Betty, my maid, popped her head round the door carrying a bowl and some linen towels. "I have some hot salt and lavender water to dress my lady's wounds."

"Good, good." My father, Thomas, stared hard at me. "Do not waste your time chasing boys my sweet. Trust me on this."

The heavy wooden door slammed behind him and I heard his booted footsteps clatter downstairs to my mother in the kitchen.

I flinched as Betty bathed my cuts, the more I squealed, the more she pressed the salt into my blooded backside. "You're doing that on purpose." I snapped at her, sounding just like my mother.

"No, mistress, sorry mistress." She carried on ignoring my protests as she worked. The lavender cream was cold on my buttocks but soothing. "I'm going now mistress." Her skirts rustled on the floorboards as I heard her get up. I didn't turn around. I was embarrassed enough for one day. I did not want to see her laughing as she clattered her way out of my room. Off downstairs to tell the other maids what I had been about.

"What are we going to do Thomas?" Mother was sitting by the window using the last of the fading light to stitch black-work berries onto her new coif. "She will lead us into disgrace, she doesn't know right from wrong, despite all my scoldings and teachings." Her needle moved swiftly as blackberries and their leaves appeared on the white linen under her thin fingers. She pulled out more black silk thread from the skein. Her nails were clean and long, a luxury that showed she was neither a housemaid or cook.

Thomas dropped into his favourite chair opposite his wife. “Let us send her to your sister Susannah in Oxford,” he sighed. “Unfortunately, wife, she has inherited my lust, but not your good sense.”

“It will be a big step down for her Thomas, living in the household of a midwife.” She smiled sounding pleased, “perhaps it will put her off men.” She bit the thread, breaking it off with her teeth. “I will make the arrangements.”

I left Theobalds Palace on the following Thursday morning with my clothes press thrown onto the coach behind the footman. I left the fair, oval faced, long limbed, handsome Prince Henry strolling in the grounds. Magnificently dressed in red velvet with gold braid, a short dark purple cloak thrown carelessly over his right shoulder. A bright purple and gold beret trimmed with pearls on his royal head. He was laughing as he talked with his friends and his tutor, my father. I saw father give a backward glance over his shoulder to the carriage. I waved, I'm sure he saw me. Father turned back to the Prince and his entourage, and smiling, continued his lecture on the change of the seasons to his students.

The day had started hot and burned the dusty roads. Oxford seemed very far away to me, it was not just the road that burned. Also my bottom, and my eyes with tears, mother did not even say goodbye. It was almost as if I had died. My palace life had ended and my life as an ordinary citizen had begun. I sat in the carriage alone, as it jolted over the dusty roads. Sometimes one of my smaller boxes would fall from the seat opposite. An hour into the journey, I was sick and hot. Luckily we had stopped at an Inn for refreshment. The horses were given large buckets of water, as I watched the water slopping into the horses’ mouths, I realised I needed to piss.

At the back of the Inn were the jakes, piss pots and holes in the ground. I stood looking at them not knowing what to do when a grubby maid from the Inn grabbed my arm.

"I'll shows you milady what's about. Leaves your skirts down, put the piss pot up." With one sturdy arm, she put a pewter pot under her skirt and between her legs, steadying herself on the wall with the other arm. There was the sound of a heavy flow. "Takes it out the back careful not to drag your skirt in it, then away." She skilfully threw the green water into the hole. "Aw well, back to the kitchen." She rubbed her hands dry on her dirty grey apron.

I picked up a cold pewter pot and did as she said. Under my skirts it was impossible that the actions would be seen by anyone else. I was glad it was quiet at the back of the Inn. But I missed the hole and did drag the hem of my skirt in my water. I went to the pump and washed my hands and my skirt then clambered back into the carriage.

I was used to better things at the palace, to private closets and white china pots beneath my bed. I had wiped myself on clean rags, and washed my hands with soap made with honey and lavender. I had lost it all for a kiss on a garden seat with a Prince. However nice that was at the time, it was not worth all this. When I remembered the Prince and his lips on mine, the way his soft tongue traced my lips and caressed the inside of my mouth, I felt a thrill run through me, tingling my senses. I thought about it all the way to Oxford, giving myself little thrills until I fell asleep.

Mother told me I was allowed to eat from the basket the cook had given me. It held a big meat and potato pasty and some sweet custard tarts. There were apples, medlars, some bread and jams potted up for aunt Susannah. It also held fresh herbs wrapped in wet linen. They came straight from the gardens of Theobalds itself. After six hours, the carriage stopped at an Inn called the Star, where we were to spend the night.

As was the custom, beds were shared. I was lucky to be put with two women, one was fat and snored, the other one was thin and weaselly. I did not trust either of them. I did not get into the bed, but slept on my thick wool cloak on the floor, using my basket as my pillow. I think they were pleased not to share with a stranger. I couldn't sleep at first, noisy singing from the room below coming through the gaps in the floorboards kept me awake. I saw a mouse heading for my pasty. So I ate as much of it as I could, almost making myself sick.

I eventually fell asleep to the sounds of drunken men shouting raucously the words of a popular song. "Give me my yellow hose my friends. Give me my yellow hose, for my wife she watches me – sees everywhere I go." It was not much of a lullaby, but my bones ached from the shaking of the coach and I was full of more pasty than was good for me, so Morpheus dragged me into dreamland, whether I liked it or no.

The next morning dawned cold and overcast, the singing and the snoring had stopped, my candle had burnt out, the wax clung to the edge of my cloak. Both women were in their shifts and pissed in turn in the pot with no modesty. It turned out they were sisters. I averted my eyes. Afterwards they helped each other dress. Then washed their hands and faces, powdered their bosoms, and made their way to break their fast.

I looked at the stinking piss pots, both full to the brim. My eyes filled with tears, I wanted to go home, to clean closets, the smell of bread baking in the morning, gobbets of fried bacon and mother's posset. A lovely fresh herb drink that she squeezed orange juice into.

"Full is they?" A girl about my own age appeared through the door, she was wearing a rough wool singlet over a mud coloured shift and skirt. She came in and saw me staring at the pots. She opened the window and shouted in a loud rough voice "Garde Loo!" She threw the contents out of the window. "Full 'em up I can wait."

I crouched over the pot but strangely couldn't go. The maid went to the door turned her back on me as she whistled down the stairs. Suddenly I was all right again and the relief was immediate.

She was good at her job, she waited for me to finish and poured some water over my hands into a bowl.

Suddenly a young lad arrived with fresh warm milk, some bread and butter, and a hunk of cold bacon. He left it on the dressing table, disappearing as quickly as he came.

Her broad brown face smiled. "Get it down ye maid – talk from the coachman is ye've fallen from grace." She winked. "So did I, but I lost the babe luckily."

I didn't care any more. That people I didn't know, thought they knew me. I launched into the food with vigour as soon as she left the room. It had already been paid for, so I was going to eat it. Coming up to the age of sixteen, I was always hungry, I wasn't supposed to be, but I was.

On the last stage of the journey through the little village of Wendover, every bone in my body ached from the jolting of the coach, my clothes smelt of piss and sweat. Luckily, I did not have the large red bed bug bites on my skin as my room-mates did. But I did have flea bites round my ankles from sleeping on the floor, they itched madly and I couldn't leave them alone.

If only I'd listened to Mother and Father, if only Prince Henry could marry me. I pondered on this, promising to try and change my ways. Praying to God that the pious Prince Henry would somehow realise he couldn't live without me, and send for me, and I would be Queen. I could tell mother, I told you so Madam, you are banished from my Court! Then I would have her spanked in her shift with the carpet beater in front of the kitchen staff, and make her sit in a barrel of fleas!

It dawned on me as I frantically scratched my ankles, that Prince Henry must have known I was being sent away in the coach. Father looked back, but the Prince did not. I realised then, that I was nothing to him. My teenage fantasy of becoming Queen would never come to pass.

I watched out of the coach window as the countryside turned into little honey coloured cottages. The lanes turned into cobbled streets lined with cream stone buildings. So this was to be my new home. I was fascinated, I had never been to anywhere like this. My life had been the palaces of the King and Queen from the time I was born. I had lived in guarded rooms and corridors. Walked in well manicured gardens, always under strict control of my mother and father, unless I could escape them. Which I sometimes did.

The coach came to a stop with a sickening jolt and I heard the Coachman shout loudly in his rough sing song voice, "Oxford.... Ox.... ford. Everybody out." I got out, gathered my boxes together as they were slung from the coach by the outriders, and sat on them. I looked up, we were inside the city walls at the Cornmarket, stalls were selling bread, poultry and game.

Corn was not being sold under the covered market by the North Gate today, the harvest had not yet been gathered. The corn needed but two more weeks of sun. Men, women and children hurried by. I searched the faces for one I recognised, Oxford had been badly hit by the smallpox and many of the faces I looked at were raddled with scars.

It was four o'clock and Christchurch's Great Tom clock chimed the hour. I fidgeted, ferociously scratching the fleabites around my ankles, when I felt a gentle hand on my shoulder.

"Susannah!" I screamed, relieved to see a friendly face. "Aunt Susannah!"

Susannah was as kind as Mother was cruel. She had completely lost her Scots accent over the years, as had I, but through practice.

"My little niece." She smiled as she hugged me close. Her husband, Thomas, who was a step behind her, piled my boxes into a dog cart he was pulling. We set off hand in hand to her house in Bear Meadow chatting as we walked. It took us twenty minutes to reach her home, it being slightly out of town. It was a small cottage, having only ten rooms. They had a still, and a small dairy, a laundry fed by their own well in the garden, now covered by a circular locked wooden door. I raised my eyebrows, but Thomas explained the scholars liked to play jokes by occasionally polluting their well. The last time having put ink into it so that all their laundry and food came out blue. Susannah said it would have been funny if it had not been so destructive.

When Thomas told me that was the least worst they had put into it, I shuddered, it set my imagination running wild with possibilities.

My shoes rubbed my heels red raw, my hose rubbed my fleabites, my skirt had begun to stink of my travels and my shift was soiled. My tears had started to fall before we reached their doorstep.

"I am so filthy from the coach, I cannot go into your house like this." I sobbed looking at the open door from the neat little garden. It lead in to a good room with fresh flowers in a Delft vase on a polished walnut press. The floor was strewn with fresh clean herbs. Late afternoon sunlight shone through the open windows making shadow patterns of leaves on the walls.

Thomas laughing picked me up. "We can put you to rights young lady!" As Susannah opened the door to the laundry. I could see two housemaids of about twelve laughing and splashing about in the soapy water in the large wooden tub. They were stamping the sheets down to get the dirt out of them.

"What is happening?" I asked frightened with Susannah's husbands' strong arms around my waist. Thomas dropped me gently on the stone floor and smiled at his wife. "I will come back to see the transformation in an hour or so my dear."

He ordered the two laundry maids out to the garden into the sun. They took the sheets with them to hang over the bushes to dry.

"Yes, this is just right." Susannah tried the water with her elbow. She unlaced my bodice and untied my shift, the big bone button at the back of my skirt popped under her fingers. "Get in." She said stiffly, sounding like my mother.

I climbed the ladder - about four steps - and got into the tub in my dirty shift.

"Arms up." Susannah ordered as she pulled the shift over my head.

"It's too hot," I screeched, "it's not healthy to bathe like this!" I complained.

"My dear," my aunt took a cloth and soaped it with lavender and beeswax and cleaned my back, "the heat will kill the fleas and anything else you have living in your person." I did not know what she meant then. It was only years later that the penny dropped.

As she scrubbed away with the linen, I flinched.

"What is this?" Susannah gently rinsed the suds from my back and shoulders, old scars barely healed, and new sore ones open on my lower back. "Who did this to you?"

"Mother." I answered, I decided I quite liked the hot soapy water all over me, it was a new experience and I found I could float if I supported my head on the top step and rested. I closed my eyes. "She thinks I am very bad."

"Are you?" asked Susannah washing my hair.

"No, I try to be good. But I am never good enough for Mother." I felt tears burn. "I did nothing my dear aunt, a boy kissed me and I didn't dislike it, that was all."

"Now, now," Susannah said brusquely. "I shall go get your clean clothes and a posset. Do you like honey?"

I nodded. I decided I liked being cared for.

As I came out of the tub my travelling clothes went in. They were mainly linen and wool, I pitied the maids who would have to launder and iron them.

I sat wrapped in a white linen sheet on a wooden stool in the laundry, my skin red and sore from the heat of the water, but feeling clean and refreshed and very tired. I could hardly keep my eyes open.

Susannah came and put a cooling balm on my back, followed by my good white shift and a pale linen summer skirt. I pushed my growing bosoms into my bodice as my aunt pulled the laces tight. She gave me my scarf to cover my shoulders and paps. She pinned it together with a little pewter badge.

"What is that?" I asked looking at it

"It's a pilgrim badge." Thomas came through the door of the laundry. "You may keep it, for you have wandered far and found redemption." He smiled kindly.

"Are you a preacher?" I asked looking at him. He laughed. "Lord no, I try to be a physician. I am learning and teaching at the same time." He strode into the sunlight of the garden, three fat red hens scattered around his feet. "You are already looking much better."

"I feel cleaner." I smiled, holding my hands out to take the tankard from him.

"Here is your posset." he watched me as I sipped it. "We will see if there is anything ready for you to eat."

I followed them into the garden and sat on a small wooden bench under the apple trees, clutching the pewter tankard in my hand. It was just hot enough to hold. I drank it down, soft warm creamy milk, honey with a slightly bitter aftertaste. It was not like mothers' but I liked it well enough.

I heard my benefactors talking as they walked towards the door of their house.

"What do you think?" Susannah asked her husband.

"She seems innocent enough, the rue in the posset will expel anything got."

What have I got? I wondered drinking the warm milk.

"How long?" She asked her husband.

"By this evening, four hours we will know."

"Katherine has beaten her very badly." Susannah bit her lip to stop herself crying. "Her back is cut to pieces with old and new scars."

"I don't think she deserved that." Thomas took her hand. "No-one deserves that."

I fell asleep in a big comfortable feather bed in the small room over the kitchen. Warm with the late summer sun coming through the windows, it smelt of roasting meat and fresh bread. It was not like living in a palace, but I thought I could like it well enough. If I was really, really, good, Susannah and Thomas might even come to love me. With this comforting thought in mind I heard the church clock strike six. It was not long after that I fell asleep having had a bite of bread and butter. At last I felt safe, safe from mother. If this was a fall from grace, it wasn't too painful.

When I woke in the morning, Susannah herself came to empty my pots and bring me water to wash.

"Nothing." She whispered to her husband as she emptied them into the garden drain.

"Good." He smiled. "We'll give her another posset tonight – just in case."

The following six weeks passed in a flurry of happiness. I did not think of boys at all. I worked as well as any in the household. As I could also read and write, one of my jobs was to copy Thomas' prescriptions in a 'fair hand' so the apothecary could read them. I was soon set tasks of taking messages into Oxford and doing the household accounts.

Suddenly I found myself very important indeed!

On the eighth week something extraordinary happened that changed my life.

"Anne." Susannah called for me from the sitting room. I raced in to see Susannah and Thomas smiling at each other and holding hands. My heart sank, perhaps they were sending me away – perhaps I had overstepped my authority.

"Worry not." Thomas looked at my sullen face. "For 'tis good news." He looked across at Susannah, smiling. "Shall I tell her?"

She nodded.

"We have bred, at long last after three years of marriage, we have bred!" He grinned.

"You have brought us luck!" Susannah pulled me forward. "I want you to learn my trade, I want you to help deliver the child with my gossips."

"Me a midwife?" I was aghast.

"Yes you, are you not excited?" She smiled. "We felt the babe quicken last night, so now we can tell the world." Susannah skipped a little.

"Do you feel well?" I asked, really not knowing what to ask.

"Really well, and so happy, you have lightened my load so much Anne that I am able to breed! Thank you." She hugged me tightly.

I felt a little jealous of the little creature inside my aunt, the baby would have a loving mother and father. I had a loving father who I missed, and a mother who I desperately wanted to love me, but didn't.

"We are a proper little family now," Thomas smiled handsomely, pleased with himself, "that includes you too Anne." He picked up his leather snapsack, full of his instruments, from the table. "Well ladies I must away to my business, and you to yours." He kissed his wife, chucked me under the chin and walked out into the garden where the boy was waiting with his horse.

The boy looked puzzled as Thomas tousled his hair and leapt onto his horse, a fine black stallion called Mighty, that Thomas had been given as a wedding present by his father.

When he left Susannah and I were alone in the parlour.

"May I ask you something aunt?" I asked sitting on the settle.

"Of course Anne, anything." She smiled as she sat beside me.

"Did you marry Thomas because he had the same name as my father or because he was kind like my father?" I asked taking her hand.

She smiled at her teenage niece's silly questions. "Both, I suppose. My mother, your grandmother, arranged the marriage. She did a good job, I am very happy." She gave a little giggle. "Perhaps my mother only had takings for men called Thomas, so married both her daughters to one!"

It was coming on to autumn, the leaves were starting to turn gold, amber and red as I turned sixteen. The blue sky was shredded with fine white clouds and Oxford, as always, was busy. I was to take a script to the apothecary, have it made up, then go to Trinity College and give it to a master there. Then collect the money, pay the apothecary on the way back and put whatever was left in the strong box in Thomas' surgery. I had done this many times before, I liked to be sent on messages. I would walk through St. Giles with my head held high, I was wearing my new brown felt hat over my coif. I had bought myself a white scarf trimmed with Honiton lace with money father had sent me. Guilt money for sending me away - I suspected.

I felt important, I had a family, a good family, and I think, well hoped, they loved me. I liked living in Bear Meadow, a little hamlet just outside Oxford city walls. I would look in the shops in the town, and watch the wealthy handsomely dressed students carrying their books in leather straps as they wandered through the streets in their black gowns chatting about their lives. I wondered why there were no young women students. Oh yes, we are to feed and breed, we have no other course but that. No-one likes a clever woman, it makes us evil and manipulating. According to the Bible it was Eve that led

Adam into trouble in the first place.

I went to the apothecary's shop opposite Trinity College for no other reason than he was the only person to give Thomas credit when he and Susannah moved to Oxford. I loved the perfume of the herbs and tinctures as I opened the door and went in.

"Hello again – young Anne, always a pleasure to see you." He screwed his eyes up at the paper I had given him, and a smile crinkled the side of his lips. Mr Whipp was in his forties, fairly rotund, with brass circular spectacles, his wiry hair was greying at the temples. "Not your writing is it? Oh it was such a relief to me when you came to your aunt and they gave you the job of re-writing Thomas' scripts, his writing is truly awful."

"Can I read it to you – I am quite good at deciphering his writing." I took the paper and stood by the light of the window, I traced the pen marks with my finger. "He is asking for St John's Wort, a tincture of rose leaves not petals, and rosemary. Also in a separate paper six senna pods."

"Ha, we have a melancholic to treat." Mr Whipp busied himself with his pottery jars. "This will be quite expensive, may I ask who the patient is?"

"No you may not Mr Whipp, for if I tell you, you will treat him direct and Thomas will lose his living. You try me hard with this every time, give it up!" I laughed.

"Well, well maid, I wish I had a helper half as sharp as you." He smiled as he handed me a small round pottery bottle with the tincture, a paper cone folded at the top with the senna pods, on it he had written 'one a day in Rhenish wine to purge the humours and a handful of dried leaves.

"Thank you Mr Whipp I shall bring the money directly. How much should it be?" I put the medicines in my leather pouch.

"A shilling." He smiled leaning back amongst his tinctures.

"A shilling?" I gasped, shocked – "that is a maids wage for a year, can I give anything back?"

"Charge two shillings, believe me, whoever it is can pay. This is Oxford after all, and it is not cheap to live here. No, the melancholic will need everything – you are not the Physician after all." Mr Whipp dismissed me with a frown.

I walked to Trinity College to find the Don who had ordered the medicines, I didn't get past the gatehouse, a runner was sent to find him. An elderly man with thinning white hair in a tattered black gown appeared with a worn-out pouch that jingled as he made his way towards me.

"Yes, yes," he snapped, "who are you?" He stared at me through watery blue eyes, he must have been a hundred if he was a day.

"Thomas the physician sent this over for you." I got out the bottles and the packages and my uncles' badly written instructions, and passed them to the old man.

"Well, well," he screwed his eyes up to read Thomas's scrawl.

"I can read it for you, I understand his writing." I watched his face.

I stood in the shade watching the trees of Trinity's Wilderness wave in the breeze that was starting to pick up.

"So you can read, a young woman who can read." He looked up at me. "Who taught you?"

I told him. Mother and Father were tutors to the Royal children, I could see he was impressed. He smiled a gummy smile at me. "Good, good, how much?"

"Two shillings?" I asked embarrassed.

"Is it two shillings or is it not?" He snapped rifling for the coins.

"It is." I took the money and put it in my pouch.

"You are strange." The old man said as he shambled away, his yellow hose draping round his ankles as the ties of his breeches had come undone.

"Why?" I asked puzzled, he turned and stared short-sightedly at me through the leaves blowing across his path.

"You can read, you appear clever, you are not fashionable, and yet you are of the middling sort. Also," he paused, "a young woman. Nothing about you makes sense."

I suddenly felt self -conscious enough to call after him as he shambled along the gravel.

"Is that bad?"

He turned, the wind blowing his cloak and white hair wildly about and throwing a few leaves in for good measure.

"No, no," he muttered turning away, then undecided muttered. "perhaps."

Three weeks later I helped attend my first birth, my aunt Susannah was the chief midwife and she had three gossips and myself. The lady was the Queen's Laundress who was married to the King's surveyor of horses. I believe they called on us as we too came from Scotland. Mrs Ryder was very young about two years older than myself and Mr Ryder was about six years older. They had come to Oxford on the King's command to pick up some stallions and mares for breeding, but the coach ride had been too much for Isobel Ryder. She had decided to come to escape the hard work of the Royal laundry in her delicate condition. It was the wrong decision.

"Oh God, the wee-un – it'll not be braw." She screamed in agony as she sat in the birthing chair, twisting and turning as if she'd been tortured. Blood and water poured from between her legs. "Help me, help me." She screeched, her sharp nails tearing holes in the hand of her faithful maid Flora, as she clutched her hand tightly.

"Whas ta dae?" Flora's young urgent eyes implored us on behalf of her mistress.

"Take this and give her sips of it," Gussie, the oldest of our gossips gave the young girl a cup. "Twill help with the pain." She nodded to Susannah as she gave the girl the laudanum sweetened with blackberry juice.

"How many months mistress?" Susannah asked as she looked under the blood soaked shift. Her face showed there was little hope, but Mrs Ryder, eyes closed, calmer with the laudanum did not see.

"Five or six, she didne nae what the quickening was." Mairie, one of Mrs Ryders' ladies smiled bitchily, "Tae young."

Mary, Gussie, Lucy and myself busied about boiling water and putting lavender and rosemary in it. We folded clean linen cloths.

Susannah signalled to Gussie, "Bucket" she whispered, it was duly delivered half full of warm water, a pink slug covered in blood slid out of Mrs Ryder and into the bucket with a splash. Susannah picked it out, wrapped it tightly in a clean cloth so that just the face showed. Waxen, eyes closed, nose plugged with white stuff. There was not enough baby under the white cloth to live. Not a breath, not a cry.

"I'm sorry Isobel, the child is stillborn." Susannah looked up at the terrified young woman. "Would you like to see her?"

The scream Mrs Ryder let out was heart-rending. "Nae, take it awa. Take it awa. I've failed."

"You have not failed Isobel, we will set you to rights and you will have others." Susannah said confidently. "The air here in Oxford is not good, and you were not to know."

"Did you have a name? For we must christen the child." Gussie took the bundle and opened a glass jar of holy water.

"Marie." She choked out. She struggled upright and Gussie showed her the baby's face. If it was a boy or girl you could not tell under the swaddling, but Marie was a good enough name.

"In the name of the Father, Son and Holy Ghost, we name this child Marie Ryder, and commend her soul to God, so that she may go to Heaven and reside there until her parents join her." She dipped the child's forehead into the water and made the sign of the cross in the air as we saw the Priest do every Sunday.

It was not a proper Christening we all knew that, but we all said "Our Father," with heads bowed.

While Susannah and the gossips cleaned up Isobel Ryder I went outside into the cold air and shivered. It was not how I imagined it to be. I did not know what to expect. It was decided the child was to be put in a small coffin to be taken back to Scotland and be buried with her family. Isobel fell into a deep drugged sleep, as I cried into my hands in Broad Street in the middle of Oxford.

I remembered the oath I had signed in front of the town clerks, not to put away or dispose of a child down a well or in a ditch, not to use witchcraft during the birth, not to use any cuts or means to get the child out of the mother. Should there be a complication the husband is to decide; the mother or the child.

Susannah had told me that most husbands asked her first "Is it a boy?" If the answer was yes, then came "Save the child."

Only one man out of twenty said "My dear wife, we can have other children."

As I sat on a small stone wall outside the house with my head in my hands, in the confusion of life, I felt a gentle hand on my shoulder.

"Mistress Farthing, what causes you such distress? What?" The old Don I had been delivering the medicines for melancholy to, was standing beside me, his white hair blown about wildly in the cold breeze.

"We could not save the babe." I gave the short answer.

"Come, come, you do have some successes." He smiled offering me his hand, "Come lady and meet one." I took his bony firm hand. He led me towards Trinity College and the garden they called the Wilderness. Head down, I saw my leather shoes on the cobbles, his worn-out slippers with his grubby yellow hose crumpled over them. I could not lift my head for tears.

In the garden he led me to a wooden bench where a young tawny haired man was sitting reading. "Here he is, cured by your master's preparations, delivered by your own fair hand."

"My Lord Howard, may I introduce Mistress Anne Farthing apprentice midwife and doctor's assistant." He smiled at me as I gave a low curtsey. When I lifted my head I found I was looking at a handsome young man of about eighteen, his long fairish locks curled over his doublet collar. His cheeks were ruddy from sitting in the chill air. When he smiled at me my stomach jumped into my mouth. He stood and gave a short bow, swooping his arm across his chest in an exaggerated movement.

"So, Mistress Farthing, my Don says you both read and write and are by far the most intelligent young lady he has ever met." He laughed, "You frighten him, if all women had your wit he says, men would quake in their breeches."

"Tut, tut Howard, what rubbish you do say." But he winked at me as he shambled away back into the warmth of the halls.

"Should he not stay?" I asked worried that my reputation, already tarnished, should take another blow.

"A chaperone?" Howard laughed, "My dear look about you, every window has a face in it, every gardener works on the lawns, there is no privacy here."

"You do not seem melancholy my Lord." I watched his handsome face, his smile was bright as his blue eyes sparkled at me.

"Not now you are here." He grinned. "I am reading Virgil in the Latin, that is enough to make any man miserable."

"I am learning Latin so I may help write and read prescriptions." I smiled at him, "I am not very good yet." I watched him shift to pull his Dutch coat on over his shoulders. He was well formed and looked to have strong arms and shoulders.

He dropped his book. I picked it up without thinking.

"You have had a bad day Mistress." He took the book, dusted off it's brown leather cover and put it on his lap. "Why?"

"How do you know that?" I asked puzzled.

"My dear old master brings me people who are worse off than I, in a bid to cheer me up."

"Oh," I shivered. "Does it work?"

"Sometimes." He smiled. "Now you, what happened to you?"

I told him. He mused on my words for a moment.

"Why are you melancholy My Lord?"

"It is a blackness that visits me, I understand why they call it the Black Dog, for it is ever faithful and hardly ever leaves my side."

He explained that ever since he was a child he had moments of despair so deep that not even his mother or his nurse could lift him out of it.

There were days, sometimes even weeks at home, when he could laugh with his friends and make merry. Since he had come to Oxford to study, there were hardly any days where he was free of the misery, the Black Dog had followed him and sat beside him every day.

"Perhaps," I mused to myself, "you need more amusement than study. Many of the young men hereabouts ride, gamble, hunt game and what not. Perhaps you may need to go home for a visit – is that allowed – mayhap you are homesick?" I watched his face.

"You are a dear little thing," he grinned "could you visit again?"

"I don't know." The church clock was striking five. "I must go, my aunt will be worried."

"May I visit you?" He asked watching me stand up.

"We are a Doctor's household, not grand enough for a Lord to visit." I watched his eyes.

"That is exactly why I could visit, to thank the Doctor for his work." He stood tall beside me. "I shall walk you to the gate."

We walked together to Trinity's gate. As it clanged shut behind me I raced off down Broad Street to see if Susannah was still at the house we had been working at all afternoon. A red-faced petulant maid came to the door. "Your mistress and her gossips have gone home, she says she will see you there." She slammed the door in my face.

I raced through the streets of Oxford, ignoring the cat calls from the men standing on the street corners, to the warmth and safety of my aunt's house. I shut the door behind me and leant on it. There was the delicious smell of frying hare and fresh bread being cooked, fresh fruit sat on the table set for dinner, a grand salat had been made. I was hungry after my adventures and rushed to the kitchen to wash my hands and help put the plates on the table.

Susannah smiled at me. "All right niece?"

"Yes, I took a walk." I hugged her. "Your babe?"

"Will be as right as rain." She put out some pottery mugs by the plates. "I am after all married to a Doctor." Then as an afterthought. "Who truly loves me."

I visited Howard many times over the coming weeks, not just to deliver his medicine, but because it gave me pleasure to be in his company. We would find a quiet spot in the grounds to sit and talk and when it was cold we would creep up to his rooms.

"How came you by the name Farthing?" He asked one day, "Tis unusual, tis definitely not Scots."

Howard sipped the warm posset I had made for him and stared into the flickering fire in the grate.

"My Grandmother made farthingales for Queen Mary of the Scots, and then for Queen Anne." I sighed, "Queen Mary jokingly called her Mrs Farthingale thinking it was funny that one of the Royal mistresses of the wardrobe should be named after her underwear."

Howard tutted.

"My grandfather was a Scots Guard of the Queen, he took this humiliation badly. Especially when the Queen insisted my Grandmother change her name. When Mary died, Grandfather was pleased. He said beheading was too good her. They changed the name to Farthing as they still worked for the Royal court, and my Grandmother continued to make clothes for Queen Anne until she died."

Howard whistled through his teeth. "That is some tale. Shame you weren't called McFarthing!" He laughed.

"I don't think that was allowed." I grinned. I looked out of the window, "I must go, it's getting dark."

"May I walk you home?" He asked kindly picking up my heavy wool cloak and handing it to me.

He finished his drink swiftly and put his doublet on, topped with a half cloak. It was getting colder as the sun had set.

"People will say we are courting." I stood up and straightened my skirts. I swung my cloak elegantly over my shoulders.

"I wish we were." He held my cold hand in his warm one. "You are the only person I feel I can be myself with, tell secrets to, kiss in all innocence."

I helped him with the many small Dorset buttons on his doublet. "You are already promised, your Don told me you are to be married to Lady Winterton."

"My parents choice, not mine." He bent down to pick up his velvet cap. "It matters nothing to them that I care not for this lady. What does matter is her large dowry, and the manor house that accompanies it." We walked arm in arm towards the door. "Her parents want her wed, they are old and want to hand the running of the manor and estates to a younger body. I swear it is not for me Anne. I would marry you if you had a dowry of two mites and lived in a pig sty."

I laughed, it sounded hollow in the grand hall as we passed through. "Oh Howard if only we were two different people of the same class, what fun we could have."

The candles flickered and gushed in the wind as we opened the door to the street, already growing pitch black. A few scholars with lanterns were hurrying home to their firesides.

"Will you come again tomorrow my dear?" Howard asked as our shoes clattered down the cobbles of Broad Street. An icy blast took my cloak and I wrapped it round me again quickly. The clasp was wearing out and I could not afford to buy a new one.

"I wish I could but my mother and father are to visit us, and it is a long way from Theobalds Palace, and I dare not disappoint them." My cloak clasp fell undone again.

Howard wrapped the cloak around me, and despite his best efforts to fix it, I had to hold it closed as we rushed through the bitter cold streets to Bear Meadow.

"You have saved my life sweet Anne." Howard smiled as we reached the door of Aunt Susannah's house. "How will I manage without you for even a day?"

He pulled me close to him and kissed me on the lips again and again. "Remember my love, come as soon as you can."

"I will," I smiled happily as the naughty wind wrenched the heavy wool cloak from my hands. It made Howard hold on to his cap as he raced away through the darkened streets back towards St. Giles and Trinity.

Once past the garden gate I looked up into the black starry sky, snowflakes were starting to fall, whirling prettily in the wind. I closed my eyes and stuck out my tongue, like a child playing. The cold salty snowflakes melted in the heat of my mouth. I smiled as I hurried through the garden to the front door, I opened it to a welcoming roaring fire in the hearth. Susannah sat on the settle warming her feet, the woman sitting beside her stood up.

"Anne!" Mother's voice pierced the warmth and happiness of my home with ice. "Where in Heaven's name have you been?" Her eyes looked me up and down spitefully.

"Trinity College mother, delivering medicines." I curtseyed as I spoke. I held out my arms to embrace her. She knocked my cloak away from my stomach, to see if I was with child, but as the clasp was broken it fell to the floor. I quickly picked it up. "How can you abide her Susannah?" she asked turning her back on me.

Father came and embraced me instead. "You must be freezing Anne, come sit by me, here by the fire."

I sat on the settle beside him watching Mother's jealous eyes as he rubbed the warmth back into my hands. "We came early, are you pleased?"

"Yes father, I wish I had known, I would have tried to get back sooner." I stood up. "I must go and wash my hands and face." I picked up my cloak and put it in the clothes press on my way to the kitchen, mainly to show mother my trim figure and flat stomach. I hurried into the kitchen where our two fat hens were roasting on a spit in front of the fire, and warm fresh bread sat on the table waiting for our guest's dinner. I poured water into a bowl and washed the soot and dirt from the streets off me. I used the lavender and honey soap that I had made myself.

I had made gifts for Mother and Father, I ran quickly to my room to fetch them. I took them out of my sewing box. I had been preparing for their visit for weeks, as soon as Susannah had told me they were coming for Michaelmas.

"Mother, Father," I curtseyed before them on the settle, "I have a gift for you. I have made them myself." I gave mother a piece of linen wrapped around her gift. "I hope you like it, it's very fashionable in Oxford."

She opened the linen and saw a beautifully made frog purse, with green beads for eyes, the mouth tied shut with gold cord, it's legs made of twisted dark green wool around twigs.

"Oh," she gasped surprised, "What do you think Susannah?" showing it to her sister.

"It's beautiful." Susannah smiled at me, "You must have worked hard."

"You have it then." Mother passed the little frog to her.

"No, sister, she made it for you." Susannah looked upset.

"Oh I have no need of such things, if it's fashionable in Oxford, it should stay here." She looked away from us both into the fire, and started to warm her hands.

Tears started to fill my eyes, Father noticed. "What about me?" He smiled lovingly. "What have you made me?" I gave him his present.

"Tis a case for quills and chalk and charcoal, it wraps up neatly so you can carry everything you may need to teach." I felt choked, but tried to be cheerful for my father. "See I have even put in a little bottle of ink which I have made myself."

"My dear girl, you never fail to surprise me, Susannah tells me you are learning Latin, making medicines, and now this beautifully made wallet for all my necessaries." I hugged him. "I am a good girl father, I promise." Suddenly I was a little girl again, wanting to be loved.

"Are we never to eat Susannah?" Mother snapped nastily.

Trinity Halls, Oxford. January 1611

After Christmas, Howard and I became closer. His impending marriage to Lady Winterton had been arranged for May of the next year, on hearing this, his Black Dog had returned with a vengeance.

I had been called to his rooms by his old Don who had sent an urgent message via Mr Whipp. Although unasked, Mr Whipp insisted on coming with me to deliver the medicines.

Howard was lying on his bed, he had been crying. He had a pistol in his hand.

"What's this? What's this?" The old man asked worried.

"I'm a coward, I can't even kill myself." Howard's face crumpled with tears.

I wanted to go and hold him to me, but with the Don and Mr Whipp present I knew it was not possible. I had just seen him a few days before, he was low, but not like this. I had held him in my arms, rocking him to and fro, nursing him like a babe. Trying to comfort him, telling him I would always be there for him. His eyes were bloodshot, his handsome face distorted with a pain none of us could see.

"I'll fetch Dr Thomas Goode," I turned to go, feeling sick with worry.

"No! No!" Screamed Howard. "Send my Don, I need you here."

Mr Whipp looked at me puzzled. "Did you bring the medicines I gave you?" He asked. "Let us mix a potion to give this young man relief before the Doctor comes with his leeches."

We walked to the broad window sill so that we could work in the daylight. Howard's anxious eyes followed our every move. Mr Whipp took the packages I had bought from him, added a tincture of something from a green bottle in his pocket. The light from the window lit the medicines through the glass and their colours reflected on the walls.

Howard screamed. "Will this never end? God, I pray you, make an end of me." He struggled upright holding his head, his eyes wide and bloodshot. I went to him and put my arms around his shoulders. "Tell me where is the pain?"

He whispered in my ear, "Tis you, tis leaving you."

I don't know if Mr Whipp heard, but he gave me a nostrum for Howard that I made him drink for me. In a few moments, red faced and breathing heavily he was asleep.

"He relies on you too much." Mr Whipp took off his spectacles and cleaned them with his handkerchief. "I have seen it before. The relief from the drugs we make that gives him the false idea that it is you, not them, that does the work."

I took a face cloth and dipped it in the cold water on the night stand, "May I wash his face Mr Whipp? Should we take the heat out of him?"

He nodded in agreement.

"I have very sharp hearing." He stared at me. "What's been going on between our young Anne and this tortured soul here?"

"We talk. When I deliver his medicines." I watched Howard's face. "In fine weather we walk the grounds hereabouts, we talk of everything. I read to him sometimes."

"So you are courting?" Mr Whipp put his spectacles back on.

"Is that courting?" I asked, knowing full well it was more than friendship. I had loved Howard from the moment I had met and talked with him on that dreadful day of the birthing of poor Isobel Ryder.

"He thinks it is." Mr Whipp held a small mirror to Howard's lips. "Good, he's breathing steadily now."

Thomas burst through the door, "How is he?" He stared at the patient and then at us. "Do neither of you have any sense?" He asked angrily picking the pistol from Lord Howard's hand and throwing it out of the window. "Anne, go home. This is no place for you. Pick up the pistol and take it to Susannah, she'll lock it away." He turned to Mr Whipp. "Now Sir, what have you administered?"

I walked into the quad, the old Don was holding the pistol with tears in his eyes. He was out of breath having run to fetch the doctor. I took the pistol from him and hid it in my snapsack. "Dr Goode tells me I have to take it and have it locked away."

"Quite right. Quite right." He breathed heavily.

"Do you need assistance Sir?" I asked, his face was deathly white.

"No." he gasped. "I will mend. Off you go now."

I didn't look back. I walked out of the gate onto Broad Street, my head spinning. The walk home disappeared under my feet. It seemed that in just a moment I was holding Susannah close to my chest and sobbing on her shoulder.

The following weeks were hard, and not just because the weather had set in. Crunching my way through the snow to Trinity took longer than the usual twenty-five minutes I could race. I heard Old Tom strike the hour, I had been walking for forty minutes freezing and heartbroken.

I was known by now. The gates were opened for the young lady who delivers Mr Whipp's medicines. I made my way to Howard's rooms. He was asleep on his bed, freezing cold. I put a blanket over him and lit the fire in his room. He seemed to be doing everything he could to make himself feel worse. I crouched by the fireplace striking the flints together to make a spark, my heart heavy. In four months my love would be gone. What would I do then? We had never made love in the conventional sense. We had sat together, talked, laughed, held each other and kissed, but there had been no straying hands on his part. He had never asked me for my favours. I choked back a sob. Perhaps Mr Whipp was right in his assessment of us.

The fire sparked into life and I blew the tinder to make it catch. I hung the kettle from the metal bar over the flames. It would take a while to heat. I noticed he had even opened the windows, so I closed them. Using the light from the day and the reflection from the bright white snow I mixed the medicines as I had been shown.

The room was starting to warm, and Howard was starting to wake. He turned over and watched me, a feint smile crossed his lips.

"So, I am not dead yet Anne."

I looked up at him and smiled, hoping he wouldn't see the tears in my eyes.

"Where there's life there's hope. You have been doing all you can to end it."

The kettle was hissing, it would be warm enough to make the Chinese drink. I mixed the brown herbs with the hot water and strained them off and gave it to him.

He pulled himself up. He had been sleeping in his clothes. He stank, all young men who do not wash for days, have a very distinctive smell.

"You need your servants, where are they?" I made myself a Chinese drink as I spoke. "I suppose you dismissed them?"

He nodded.

I sat on the chair beside the bed, holding my nose over my cup.

He laughed, he actually laughed. I was so shocked, I jumped out of my skin.

"Is my stench that bad?"

"Yes, you do not smell like a Lord." I sipped my tea.

He drank his in one go. "Then wash me." He stood up and took off his shirt, under the arms were hard and brown with dried sweat.

I poured some warm water into the brown pottery bowl on the dressing stand and put some soft soap into it and foamed it up.

"Aren't you cold?" I asked watching him.

"No, something in you warms me." He walked towards the fire, the room was warming up nicely now. As he bent to throw a log onto the fire, I admired his fine shape, broad muscular shoulders with a small tight waist.

"It is the fire that I made that warms you. Not I." I said watching his face. I walked towards his clothes press in the corner of the room to pull out a clean heavy linen shirt, some clean slips, his breeches and a belt. I walked back to put them over the chair by the fire to warm them through.

As I turned from my task towards the fire, I saw him naked in front of it, washing himself.

"If I were to get you with child, I would have to marry you." He grinned at me. "We would be together forever. What do you think?"

"I think I would be sent away as soon as possible and you would be hurried into the marriage that you dread." I couldn't stop looking at him, wanting him to touch me. Reluctantly I kept my place as I warmed his clothes in front of the fire for him.

"You don't know that." He grabbed my shoulders, pushed me against the wall and kissed me passionately. His hands moved swiftly up under my skirts. I wanted him, of course I did, but good sense prevailed. I pushed him away.

"Howard, my love, not like this."

He moved away. "You are right, of course you are. We must do this properly."

"What do you mean?" I asked handing him his shirt.

He pulled on his slips and breeches and tucked the shirt in. He fastened the belt around his trim waist. "I will write to my parents to ask if I can wait a year or two before the marriage. Complete my education in Paris, Rome and Venice. When I return I will be in my age of majority. I can marry who I like."

"Really?" I smiled, for the first time in months, I had seen a glimmer of hope on his face. Hope is a dangerous beast, it promises all, to sometimes deliver nothing.

"Will you wait?" He asked, grabbing my hands and pulling me to him.

"Yes," I kissed his hands, "will you?"

He picked me up to swing me round. He flung me on the bed and lay on top of me, his muscles hard against my soft body.

Suddenly the door swung open. Howard's master stood open mouthed looking at us. His eyes narrowed in anger.

"Get out." He snapped sternly at me. "Now."

I wriggled out from under Howard, he stood up in front of me. "It was just horseplay, master, the maid is still a maid."

The old Don licked his lips with a thin tongue. "I am not so old that I cannot tell what is what boy. Your parents and Lady Winterton are on their way up." He looked at me. "Get your cloak on and collect his washing, pretend you are a servant, tidy, make tea, whatever servants do." He clicked his tongue. "If the world was how I would like it, I would see you and Howard married tomorrow." He wound his thin hand round my arm. "Believe me."

I put out cups, made some more of the Chinese herb drink that uncle Thomas had bought us from London. The old Don found a linen sack for me to put Howard's dirty clothes in. I busied myself while the old Master went to fetch Lord Howard's party waiting downstairs.

I curtseyed to the party as the door opened. Howard's mother was a stunningly beautiful woman for her age, her golden hair curled in ringlets around her unlined face. Her skin smooth, unblemished. Howard's father was tall and broad, a hail fellow well met, type of man. Pleased with everything, especially the improvement in health of his son.

"You are well?" He asked shaking Howard by the hand.

"Thanks to Mistress Farthing, my dear Don, Dr Thomas Goode and Mr Whipp, they have all worked miracles." Howard showed the party to the seats we had pulled in from other rooms and arranged by the fire. The last of the party was a pinch faced woman, about three years older than Howard, with a thin, mean little mouth. She looked around Howard's rooms with distaste.

"What on earth is that dwedfall smell?" She lisped. "Is it you?" She looked directly at me.

I lowered my face to hide my smile. "No my Lady, 'tis my Lord Howard's laundry."

"D' you smile at me madam?" She asked, dropping her cloak to show a tiny waist to match her tiny mind.

"No my lady, to be sure, I will take it away." I curtseyed to all, then dragged the linen bag out with me.

"Damn pretty gel, what?" Howard's father grinned as he watched me leave. "You spoil yourself my son, with your servants."

Howard turned to his father. " She is the Doctor's assistant, she brings my medicines to me from the apothecary Mr Whipp."

"Good man Whipp," Howard's father smiled. "Heard good things. What is this brown brew she has made?"

"It is the Chinese drink all the rage in London." The old Don passed the cups round. "It's called tea. Her master Dr Goode recommended it to your son as a pick me up."

Howard's father sipped it. "God's teeth, 'tis foul, this will never catch on."

Lady Winterton lisped, "I quite like it. I will order thome if it's all the wage in London."

Howard turned to his old Don and rolled his eyes to the ceiling. The old man smiled gently.

Oxford, Mayday 1612

After a wet early Spring, at last the fields and gardens were coming to life. Susannah and Thomas' first child had been born. A boy. Both were well pleased with the situation, even if I was not. Who knew that babes could be so troublesome? If it was not crying to be fed, or changed, or colic, or teething, it was for attention. Which both over loving parents provided in abundance. As for me, it left me no peace to read the letters from my dear Howard. He was in Venice, enjoying the culture, and the women no doubt. Tho' he made little mention of that. His father had sent him on his tour with his cousin Rafe, whom I had never met. I instantly disliked him, having a name I believed, which was made for trouble.

I folded the letter carefully and put it in my writing box. Susannah had bought me the box. It was a very expensive gift for my helping to deliver her son. He, at that time, had slipped into the world almost painlessly for her. It having had nothing much to do with my skill or lack thereof.

As we heard the May morning hymns being sung from the towers in Oxford, I felt a little thrill in my heart. I knew that later in the day the Maypole would be raised in the town centre, Morris men would dance, the Green Man would make an appearance. There may be dancing and music and I dearly hoped that I could find a partner, other than my dear brother-in-law, to dance with this year.

The young girls who served our household had bedecked their hair with any flowers they could find. They had dressed in their best clothes, with brightly coloured ribbons lacing their bodices and shoes.

Susannah sighed watching them as they giggled together down the lane.

"What are you thinking?" I asked her, watching her sad face.

"That Tabby and Barbara will soon want husbands of their own and leave me. Tabby was eight when I pulled her out of the derelict buildings of the tanneries and butchers behind Christchurch. Poor Barbara was nine when Thomas pulled her drunk father out from between her legs at the back of the Castle Inn."

I looked at her shocked. I hadn't realised. I thought they had been servants bought from their parents in the usual way. The custom was that parents were paid their children's wages until they came of age, then the children stayed in service or went their own way in the world.

Tabby and Barbara were always laughing and happy together, now coming towards sixteen, marriageable age, Susannah thought she would lose them.

"They are like my family." She smiled watching them skip happily down the lane, their bright ribbons blowing in the breeze as they made their way towards the Mayday celebrations. "I hope they will stay, but time will tell."

Susannah turned to me. "And what of you niece? Do you still wait on Lord Howard?"

"I promised him I would." I smiled up at her.

"Hope is a dangerous emotion." She took my hand and led me to the hall mirror. "Do not rely on it." She took some flowers from the vase, starting to thread them through my hair and her own.

"We look like sisters do we not?" She smiled looking in the mirror. "Here, have some rouge, not too much, that's right on the apples of your cheeks. I have lip wax also. Quickly let us get ready before my baby wakes up and the nurse finds she cannot quiet him."

Thomas was waiting at the door, looking handsome in his new finery.

"My beautiful wife and my beautiful niece." He crooked his arms and we each took one to walk into town.

The town was busy with happy laughing people, everyone in their best clothes, Mois du May played loudly from musicians in the street. We walked among the stalls. Ribbons, silk flowers, pies, beers, cheeses, pottery, linens were all for sale. The loud jolly chatter of the crowds almost drowned out the music. The market was full to bursting with goods all pretending to be the best of this or that. The market traders sang bouncy tunes about their goods to the sound of the hurdy gurdy. In a happy mood, I tried on a reed hat I'd taken a fancy to - with a green and white ribbon.

I turned to Susannah. "What do you think?"

"Lovely." She smiled, "I might get one as well for gardening." She picked up one with a dark green ribbon and tried it on, she looked very handsome in it. We paid for our hats and wore them immediately feeling very prosperous.

"Bah," an old woman in black stinking rags stood looking at us weighing us up. "Yous know nothing, wearing green is bad luck on Mayday. Her bright dark eyes looked us up and down. Tell your fortune ladies?" She grabbed Susannah's clean white hand in her black grime covered one. Susannah pulled her hand away quickly. "Go away old woman, leave us to enjoy our day off."

The old woman grabbed my hand and opened my palm, her eyes almost disappearing under her wrinkly nut brown face.

"What do you see?" I asked watching her.

"I don't see a sixpence. Is what I don't see." She held my hand painfully tightly.

"I only have three pence."

A smile broke through her filthy face showing broken brown teeth. "Liar."

"Take it or leave it." I tried to pull my hand away.

"Don't be hasty young'un." She traced her nail, ingrained black with dirt, across the lines on my palm. "You will be crossed in love. Not once but twice." She spat into the road, she'd been dribbling as she read my palm. You will have one child. She looked up at me. But not by him." She stared at a strange man behind my shoulder, "you will live a long life, but it won't be a happy one."

"That's enough you old bitch, leave these ladies alone." A strong man's voice came from behind me.

"Pay, or I'll curse thee." She spat at me.

I put three pennies in her dirty old hand. I desperately wanted to go and wash her stink from me. I ran through the throng to the pump and washed my hands as best as I could. When I looked back towards Susannah it seemed the old woman had vanished into the crowd.

Thomas and Susannah were talking to the stranger and laughing together, it seemed they knew him. I walked back shaking the water from my hands.

"Anne, this is Colonel Arthur Windybanks, he's an old friend of Tom's." Susannah smiled. "Colonel Windybanks, this is my niece, Mistress Anne Farthing."

He bowed graciously as I curtseyed. "My absolute pleasure." He smiled. "Your brother-in-law tells me he is forced to dance with you every May Day. Would you care to change your partner and dance with me?"

I stared at Thomas, "Forced?" I asked smiling, "Am I so awful a dancer?"

Thomas blushed from his collar up, looking at Susannah for help.

"No, no." She smiled. "We have but one man between us so it is only right to take turns."

"Now you have another man to dance with, and I will dance with you both." Colonel Arthur Windybanks swept a low bow and excused himself. "Until tonight then at The Bear in Alfred Street."

Thomas laughed. "He's a likeable rogue, but a rogue nonetheless."

"What does he do?" I asked intrigued.

"At the moment he is a messenger for the King. Most trusted." Thomas put his arm around Susannah's waist, he was getting merry on all the ales he had tried.

"I wouldn't trust him." I decided as we walked through the throng to watch a juggler and some acrobats. "He seems Artful to me."

Ever since then, he became Artful to me, in more ways than one.

We went back home to change for the evening's festivities, at eight o'clock we walked together arm in arm, laughing and joking towards The Bear Inn. When we arrived it was already full to bursting. We gave our tankards to Thomas who fought his way to the taps to get them filled. Fiddle and hurdy gurdy music filled the air, and couples were reeling and dancing to one of the most popular songs.

Susannah was looking around through the smoke to see if there was anyone she knew. She waved at Gussie, one of her gossips, she was sitting on her husband's lap as there were no seats left to be had. Considering the substantial size of Gussie and the smaller size of her husband, I was surprised to see that when she stood up to greet us, he wasn't squashed flat.

Room had been cleared for dancing in the middle of the Inn. The drums soon had my feet tapping as the Oxford Waites fiddled, sang and drummed out their tunes. Everyone collapsed into laughter at the end of the reel and couples started to form circles of eight, man, woman, man, woman, arms about each others shoulders. I joined a group with Artful, Susannah, Thomas, with Gussie and her husband John. The blacksmith Eddie, a well built smiling young man, dragged a giggling Barbara to join us. The music bounced us up and down and we danced to the left and then to the right, then something unexpected happened. Artful smiled at me whispering “Lift your feet mistress!” as the dance got faster and the men reeled round, the ladies became like spokes of a cartwheel.

Many of the ladies were supported by our linked arms to each other, resting on the shoulders of our men we were whirled off the floor. I had never seen or taken part in such a dance. The music grew faster more frantic, my outstretched legs were now at shoulder height. Even Gussie was prone in flight! I wondered how it would end, I imagined a pile of ladies in all corners of the Inn. The music slowed, and so did we, gently coming down to earth until our feet touched the ground again. The music stopped, we all bowed and curtseyed to each other then made our way giddily to collapse near our drinks.

'I wish you had have been with me.' Howard read my letter in bed in Venice. He smiled. The naked young Italian beside him got up went to the balcony to piss over the side into the canal. Afterwards he pulled his clothes on and held out his hand. Howard gave him some gold, slapped the young man's shoulder. “Addio amante.” He smiled, as he carried on reading my letter feeling a little homesick.

Bear Meadow, Oxford 1614

I lay on my bed crying into my feather pillow. The letter that I had longed for and expected from my Lord Howard had been intercepted by my mother. He had the decency to write to my father and ask for my hand in marriage. Mother took the letter and made enquiries at court, it seemed Lady Winterton's mother and father were very influential, and not to be crossed.

Howard's family wrote to my parents to ask them to keep me away from him. He was to marry a rich heiress to redeem the family fortunes, not the penniless daughter of tutors.

Mother wrote a scorching letter and told me on no account was I ever to see Howard again.

I walked broken hearted as I made my way to Trinity on the day we were to part company. We were to meet in the old orchard known as the Wilderness in Trinity College. My dear Aunt Susannah led me blindfold into Howard's arms.

I could feel his strong arms through his doublet. "This is not what I waited all these years for my love." I whispered against his cheek.

"I will find a way, we will be together my sweet one. Can you not come and live as my wife's companion?" His heart was beating fast against mine. "I can't lose you dearheart."

"That would be torture, every day near you, unable to touch you, hold you, kiss you." I sobbed, "How can you ask me that?" Hot tears fell under my blindfold. "To be with HER, not you, I couldn't stand it."

Susannah stood beside Howard's ancient white haired old Don, they turned their backs on us as we held each other tightly. Both heartbroken, we professed our love for each other as we tenderly kissed goodbye. I stroked his hair and cried into his chest. He kissed my forehead and my lips, and as he parted with his tutor by his side, he whispered. "I will never love anyone else but you."

At Susannah's house, a visitor was waiting for us when we got back, I was in no mood to speak to anyone. Thomas insisted, so red eyed and broken hearted, I sat in Susannah's beautifully furnished front room with Colonel Arthur Windybanks. He knelt in front of me and took my hands in his and kissed them.

"What are you doing?" I asked my voice broken by tears.

"I am making you a proposition. I am as you know, a spy for the King." He said proudly watching my face.

"I did not know." I answered, which was true.

"Well, I am. I am a very busy man, I need a housekeeper, and I would like it to be you." He smiled, "It would be with a view to us marrying when my work for the King is done. I would not like to make a widow of such a pretty young woman."

"What are you asking of me?" I looked across at him puzzled. He was handsome, well dressed, and always had gold in his pocket. I liked him well enough. We had met quite a few times in the past weeks at Thomas and Susannah's house for meals and to listen to music. He was witty and charming and always kissed me on the cheek before he left.

I suddenly realised I had unwittingly been courted. I burst into tears.

"I can mend your broken heart for you, if you give me a chance." He got up and stretched. "Dear lady, you may not get another offer, your reputation is sullied. Even I had to think twice before talking to you. Thomas and Susannah however have assured me you are untouched. I believe them, they are my trusted friends. Come to me, you will not regret it, I promise you."

I sat stunned for a moment, unable to speak. I looked up at Artful who had wandered to the window and was watching the late summer breeze move the field of wheat like ripples of the sea. He smiled, turning his fob watch in his fingers as I thought about his offer.

"You would not be far from your family, my rooms are in Jesus College, in Turl Street, not a quarter of the hour away." He smiled at me, "I have grown fond of you my dear."

I wept into my hands, "Not yet, for I do not know you sir. If I agree, I must have the freedom to go about my business and come and go as I please."

"Of course, I promise you that." He smiled kindly, and took my hands in his and kissed them gently.

Susannah and Thomas burst through the door, they must have been listening outside. They came in hand in hand smiling.

"Is it good news?" Susannah asked me.

"You want rid of me Aunt?" I snapped. I rushed out of the room slamming the door behind me.

"Overcome with joy." Artful smiled sarcastically at them.

It took me nearly a month to consider Artful's offer to move to his rooms. I had met him and we had talked and kissed. He made me promises I wasn't sure he would keep. Susannah's Thomas told me he was a good man, much like himself in character, and that I could do worse. It was true I did not dislike Artful, but neither did I love him. A woman on her own is prey to worse. I had more or less decided on a life of sin with him when there was a knock on my door.

"Please come down dear niece." Susannah smiled. "You are still one of the family after all."

I walked into the front room where three weeks ago Artful had propositioned me. The sun was shining brightly on the back of a tall muscular figure of the blacksmith. It was Eddie whom we had met with Barbara at the Bear Inn on Mayday.

He stood in his best clothes, nervously fiddling with his black felt hat in his hand. Susannah, Thomas and myself entered with a very excited Barbara following us. The smile she gave Eddie was sparkling.

"I should like to marry Barbara with your permission." He smiled at Thomas. "I can repay her last year's bounty with you if that's a problem." He shot Barbara a look full of anticipation.

Susannah smiled at Thomas as he answered. "You may marry without impediment. There is no bounty to pay, for no money was paid to her family as she has none. Her father died a few weeks after we took her into service."

Barbara raced to Eddies' side and grabbed hold of his broad hand as she looked up at him. "Thank you Sir," she smiled.

Susannah went to the strong box and took out some gold coins and written deeds. "We have put your pay away for such a day as this. We took the liberty of buying a small hovel on a piece of land not far from here with some of it. It is for you to start your married life in. Here is the rest." She handed over the deeds and a pouch of money. "You have worked hard, you deserve it. Don't forget us." Susannah sounded choked. Thomas squeezed her arm to comfort her.

"How could I forget you madam?" Barbara raced to Susannah's side, "You are the kindest most wonderful woman. You have been like a mother to me."

I turned on my heel to face Susannah and Thomas. "Why did you bring me to see this?" I whispered. "Am I not in enough pain that you have to torture me more?"

"But it is good news Anne," Susannah smiled warmly, "for all of us to enjoy."

Jesus College Oxford, 1625

I am still unmarried. Time has passed quickly, it is eleven years since I left Susannah's house in Bear Meadow to become the common law wife of Colonel Arthur Windybanks. I do not love him. I do not hate him. I care for him. That is all. He is gentle and kind to me. But the promise he made to me, of my marrying him, is still unfulfilled. He is always on some dangerous mission or other, leaving Oxford for weeks at a time, and I am not allowed to ask what he does. For after all, he tells me, he is a spy.

I have found that in some ways I have more freedom than I had when I lived with Susannah and Thomas in their little house. As I am on my own so much I have time to think. I quite often wonder what happened to my Lord Howard. I try not to think of him in a loveless marriage, and as much as I ask my father and mother who are close to the court. Is he happy? Does he ever think of me? Miss me? They refuse to give me an answer.

As I think back on the events that brought me to Oxford so many years ago, I find it hard to believe I am now an old maid of twenty eight. Susannah was as kind to me, as my mother was cruel, because of that I loved and respected her. She taught me her craft and so, when licensed by the town elders, I became a midwife. To follow in her footsteps to carry on her work. It did not put me off men as my mother had hoped, instead it gave me a better understanding of them.

I take my almanac and check the date, it's now 10th September 1625 and tomorrow is my birthday. I will be twenty nine. I still feel like that fifteen year old child covered in flea bites that my aunt plucked out of the carriage. I feel young. I am told I look younger than I am. My aunt is only six years older than myself, we are good friends again now. I have forgiven her for espousing me to Artful. I suppose she thought it would make me as happy as she was. I delivered her babies, and she, with the help of pennyroyal and rue, prevented mine from being born. Her husband Thomas, is still a lovely gentle man, has now become a qualified Doctor. He is kind to their children and a loving faithful husband to Susannah still.

They have a boy called Thomas; for his father and for my father, his Godfather. Two years later a girl called Tansy joined their little family. Called Tansy because when she was born her skin was as yellow as the herb.

My life in Oxford is good. I have learned a lot from the scholars and the townspeople here. However, I still miss my past days spending time with a young penniless Lord at Trinity College, called Howard. I realise now that he was my first true love. We were so cruelly torn apart from each other that he has always remained fresh in my memory. I close my eyes and I can still see his face as clearly as if it was in front of me. Sometimes I pretend he is there and reach out to stroke his tawny hair.

My current love, if you can call him that, is the Colonel. A friend of aunt Susannah's husband Thomas. Colonel Arthur Windybanks, or Artful as I jokingly call him. He tells me he is now a spy for the young King Charles who keeps him very busy.

It is he who is the father of my destroyed babes. It was he who picked up the pieces of a broken girl after her ill considered love affair with a young Lord to mend her broken heart. Hope is a dangerous emotion, do not hope. My dear Aunt told me this years ago. Despite his constant promises, Arthur and I are not married yet. He always hopes he will be able to marry me soon. I don't press him, to be honest, I no longer care. I am used to keeping my own counsel now.

He taught me the ways of men, what rises them, what pleases them. What displeases them. In return I taught him the ways of women. I cannot believe that we have been together for eleven years, the time has flown by. I keep very busy. When I moved to his small rooms in Jesus College, I ran errands for him, cooked for him, became his "housekeeper", whilst still working as a city midwife delivering babies, treating the Black Lion, and rising men up who do not like their wives.

I do not do this personally you understand. I tell them to think of rising agents. Sometimes, I give them potions of my own making, containing the stinging nettle to rub on their dogges to make them bark so to speak. I have found that some men like to be whipped. Some like to think of the young rosy buttocks of the Oxford scholars as they swim in the river Isis on a hot summers day. Some rise watching their wife's maidservant washing dishes. But once I find the trigger, rise they do, and gold coins drop into my pocket as both husband and wife are no longer displeased with each other, and of course I deliver the children.

Sometimes the Colonel would be away for weeks on end with his missions. During those times I would go back to live with Susannah in her comfortable cottage in Bear Meadow. She still kept my room for me where I always knew I was welcome. Her children, Thomas and Tansy were now coming of an age when young people usually found employment, as I had to. Thomas had no inclination, wanting to become an Oxford Scholar, but without actually having to learn anything. He walked the Oxford halls and spoke to the Scholars, drank with them, laughed with them, but did not study. Tansy was extremely vain and pretty, she had no skills apart from that, spending much of her time in front of the mirror with curling tongs, making her hair into the latest fashion.

It was while I was staying with Susannah that I found out that my Colonel was married. A message arrived at the house from his wife, she was mortal sick and needed him. It was delivered to his housekeeper for her to pass on as he was away. That was me. My father's words fell on me like hot coals. "Do not waste your time chasing boys my sweet. Trust me on this."

"Are you all right?" Susannah asked watching the colour drain from my face. I handed her the letter, she read it quietly and gave it back to me.

"You knew?" I watched her eyes. "You knew? You let me carry on with Artful?" I could feel myself shaking. "That there was no hope, never to be any?"

"Thomas told me that you knew, that Arthur told you." Susannah shrugged her shoulders, " I just thought..."

"That I was a whore? Is that what everyone else thought of me?" I could feel my temper raging, I felt sick, betrayed. "Aunt?"

She looked away her face flushed.

"You had a reputation before you came to me." Susannah went to a drawer and pulled out an old letter. She held it towards me, "Your mother told me so. Why do you think I gave you blackberry, nettle and rue to drink every day when you first came to us? So that what was created could be lost."

"Don't try to justify your actions madam." I spat at her. "I was a maid when I came here, was a maid when I fell in love with Howard. It was only Artful, it was only HE who took my maidenhead. He promised me marriage, I believed him. It was only his children that we made go to God. God forgive me." I started to shake as the floods of tears began. So no-one believed me. Not my parents, not my lovely aunt. It was probably her husband that made me prey to his best friend. I can hear his recommendation in my head now. I shuddered.

I stormed out of the house, blinded by tears. I pushed my way through the crowds in the busy street outside, I made my way towards St. Giles to go to pray on it.

It was quiet and peaceful in the church. I sat just inside the doors by the font. I thought I knew it all, yet I knew nothing. In the cool dusty silence I walked to a corner of the church and knelt in a pew and prayed. "Our father, who art in Heaven, hallowed be thy name," I whispered into my templed hands.

"Anne?" a soft cultured voice with a slight stutter that I recognised, but had not heard for years, broke the darkness.

"Charles?" I had forgotten my place as I looked at the new King. "Your Majesty, I beg your pardon."

"So, you too seek sanctuary and forgiveness." He smiled, reminding me of his brother. "I mind you, though I was only nine, dear Henry," He made a slight tutting noise trying to control his stutter, he put his finger to his lips to regain his composure. "We are both ruined in our own way are we not?"

"Sire you cannot be ruined, for you have not yet started." I gasped sitting close to him so that we could whisper together.

"We were not meant to be a King. But God chose me, a weak stuttering vessel." He smiled. "We have no choice but to make the best of it." He sighed, "Whom we are to marry, whom we may befriend, no longer mine own choice."

I wiped my eyes on the edge of my kerchief, as I listened.

"But you are married now Sire," I ventured, "we hear everything here in Oxford, married to a French Princess I believe."

He stared at me for a moment before he answered, "She is young, she is pretty. She is very argumentative. We have moved from palace to palace to escape the plague and all she does is complain." He sighed, "We are five and twenty Anne, and already tired of Kingship, for wars come upon our horizons. But for all that, we must stay, for there are others who will try to rule through us or for us." He smiled as he rested his hands on his prayer book. "My father left me a good friend, but despite our efforts and his charm, we could not gain me a wife with the Spanish Infanta. She said that she would rather go into a nunnery than marry us. So we are stuck with a French Catholic girl with a bad temper."

I stayed silent, my own problems unspoken.

"You have permission to speak Anne." He twisted his dark moustache.

"I too have been misled." I whispered. "Henry did not lay a finger on me.."

"We were only nine years old madam, we do not know what you mean."

I explained everything to him, occasionally he tutted kindly. "We think we will give you permission to marry Lord Howard."

"But he is already married is he not?" I asked half hopeful that his rich wife died a terrible death, leaving him very wealthy.

"Yes, but he is unhappy, desperately unhappy, he petitions me every week to end the marriage, as it has never been consummated. Annul it, we have the power." He leant on his silver topped cane as he got up from the pew. "What say you?"

"I am but a woman with no rights, no dreams, but I love him still." I curtseyed low as he stood. I saw him tip his hat to a man by the door.

"Anne." Howard smiled as he came towards me out of the cool dark shadows of the stone archway. Tall, handsome, his eyes shaded from the light by his black felt hat. Holding his hands out as if to embrace me.

My heart was thumping so loudly in my chest I thought everyone could hear it in the sepulchral silence of the church.

I turned toward him.

"My Lord." I smiled, as the years of pain and distrust dissolved into happiness. We held each other for a time, then the King coughed to get our attention.

"We will do this for you Anne," he smiled softly at me, "if you will do something for us."

"Anything," I smiled at Howard, drinking in his good looks, his long dark blond curled hair. He had grown even more handsome over the years, he raised an eyebrow at me.

"You speak too quick my Lady, for you do not know what the King will ask of you." He smiled holding both my hands in his as he looked at my face. I hoped I had become fair enough to still please him. I hoped he liked what he saw. "Beautiful." He whispered into my hair. "You are even more beautiful than the first moment I saw you."

"We have need of a spy." The King smiled walking between us. "We need a spy to catch a spy."

"Colonel Windybanks is not true to us." Howard lounged on a pew.

"I do not think he is true to anyone." I sat beside him.

"Up, up, for you are in the presence of the King." Charles smiled arrogantly.

We both stood, exchanging knowing looks, thinking that Charles liked this game.

"What would you have me do my Lord?" I asked. The King's face was lit by the late sun shining through the stained glass windows.

"What's to do?" Suddenly a loud voice accompanied by a strutting peacock of a man entered the silence. He glittered, wearing a white and silver doublet with matching breeches, his hat was decorated with white ostrich feathers studded with diamonds.

He strode manfully into the church. "Hey, hey, are we to put the fun into fundament?" He asked as his hand swiftly moved to my bottom and squeezed it through my skirts.

I jumped behind Howard. "I take it Sir, you are Lord Buckingham?"

In the towns and villages of England they called him "fucking him", Lord Fuckinghim. The old King's wife.

He ignored me as if I was beneath his contempt.

"Are we having this woman or not?" He moved towards me and Howard stood firm blocking George Buckingham's way. I noticed the start of syphilitic sores at the edge of his powdered mouth. He had rubbed his lips with wax so that they looked red and moist. His blond hair, curled and waved like the breakers of the sea around his beautiful face. Beautiful like a woman, but painted like a worn whore. His eyes shone a mischievous dark brown as he tried to grab me. I dodged away from him and ran for the door, he was faster and caught me. He was strong and wiry, his arm around my neck, I could feel my heart pounding in my chest. "I like the hunt." He grinned biting my ear painfully. "Hunt the c..."

"St.. St..Steenie, desist." The King shouted, "George, we need her."

He pushed me off roughly, and swaggered across to the King.

"What? This strange little creature? She is too old is she not? Ugly is she not?" He strode over to the King and leant on his shoulder like a brother. "Not for us Sire, we dislike her."

Howard put his hand on his sword. Charles frowned at him, as if to say, not here.

"We are in Our Father's House, in the presence of your Lord and King. Enough." Charles voice was irritated and fierce. He freed himself from the Duke and stood majestically in front of the rood screen facing us. "For once Sir, take heed. This maid is under our protection, she is..."

"No maid...." George laughed.

"I am as much a maid as you are." I glared at the Duke. "Perhaps you are more a Lady than I am."

Buckingham flared at this, his dark eyes flashing, he made a grab for me, he took out his sword and slashed my skirt.

Howard grabbed his arm just as he was about to hit me.

"Stop, stop." An old frail curate rushed in to see what all the noise was about. "This is the house of God."

I rushed out past him, with my latchets slipping on the cobblestones of St. Giles, I ran back to Bear Meadow. George the whore Villiers, watched me run, flushed red to his blond roots, I could hear his friend the King trying to placate him in the once peaceful chapel.

In my rooms in Susannah's house, I threw myself onto my bed and sobbed with anger. I did not understand what had happened. Although I was untouched, I felt defiled. That horrible creature had touched me. I unlaced my bodice and untied my skirt and threw them both in a corner of my room.

When Susannah came up to tell me that Artful's wife had died, she found me wearing just my shift, stamping on my clothes as if trying to kill some vermin that had invaded them.

Little Coxwell Manor, September 1625

It had taken a half days ride to get to Artful's house in Little Coxwell. He was standing in his doorway smiling as if nothing had happened. When he saw the thunder in my countenance however, his demeanour changed.

"Pretty one, precious one, what has passed?" He asked putting his arm around my waist. I shook him off.

"Liar! God's teeth, how you played me, and how you play me still." I spat at him, pulling my bags off the aged horse Susannah had let me borrow. "What am I to do now? Lay out your poor wife?"

"Jonathan" He called loudly, "Take the lady's bags inside." He looked at me frowning, I knew I was right. "I thought you'd be pleased to hear this news, and by laying her out yourself you would know I was truly free – free to marry you."

He tried to touch my hand but I snatched it away quickly to pull my cloak over my shoulders, it was starting to get cold as it got darker. "Posset for the lady," he shouted into the kitchen, where a large elderly cook was bustling about steaming pots and pans. I could smell mutton boiling – or was it perhaps a rat?

I sat in the front room of the little Manor, the fire was lit, and candles were dancing their gentle glow around the room. The heavy worn tapestry curtains had been drawn to keep out the cold. "Where is she?" I asked.

The posset was foul, my own brew much better. I threw it on the fire and it sprang into life, the alcohol feeding the flames.

Artful was shocked, he had never seen me throw a drink away. “Come this way, before the light goes completely.” I followed him up the stairs to the bedroom. Jonathan came with us and lit the candles in the room.

“What's her name?” I asked looking at the linen sheet covering her face.

“Alice. What mean you by this? What good would knowing her name do?” He pulled the sheet back, she had defecated and urinated, dried blood encrusted her mouth, her lips were blue. Her eyes open.

“It makes her a woman, like me.” I touched her marble skin, cold as ice. I had seen this before, she had been poisoned. “Has she been seeing a wise woman?” I asked as I went to the window to open it.

“How did you know?” Artful asked surprised, as a cold draft swirled round the room and left by the window. “What was that?” He shuddered his dark eyes watched the torn curtains lift.

“I have just let her soul out to go to God, it should have been done immediately after she died.” I stared at him, “This is arsenic poisoning - do you know nothing? When did she die?” I asked going to the water jug and giving it to Artful's page Jonathan.

“This morning, early.” Jonathan whispered, “She cried out and then died.”

“What did she say?” I asked handing him the water jug, “Fill this with hot water, put salt, lavender and mint in the bottom of the jug first.” I watched his young face in the flicker of the candle. “If you have none, look in the linen bag I carried with me.”

“God forgive me were her last words, that's what she said.” He took the jug and bowl away to fill it for me.

“Leave me.” I barked at Artful. “Go have your dinner, send the cook up and a maid if you have one.”

“I do not have one, there is only Jonathan and the cook, who by the way of names is called Old Barrel.” He turned on his heel and walked out.

Cold fish, I thought to myself.

"They will have to do." I shouted after him.

"Old Barry," as she preferred to be called, helped me strip and wash poor Mrs Windybanks. Her body was covered with bruises that looked like punches. Downstairs Jonathan boiled pot after pot of water so that she could be cleaned. On Alice's arms were cuts made by a small penknife. She had been fair once but streaks of grey marked the hair by her ears. She was slim and had long legs and good paps. She had never born a child, there were no stretching marks. We closed her eyes with the silver coins the Colonel begrudgingly gave Jonathan to give to us.

"Poor of 'un." Old Barry sighed, "Twas a beauty once."

"Twill be a beauty again." I went to her dresser and took out her make up. We made bandages from torn linen, and stuffed her fundament and her gillyflower with them. We managed to put a clean shift on her, but the stiffening of her body made it hard. We put her second best bodice and petticoat on, white hose and her dancing latchets with the pretty red bow. I made her face up in the current Oxford style, then I insisted that Jonathan, Old Barry and myself wash our hands and faces in hot water with the honey soap I had brought from home. We needed to wash away the bad humours from attending to her body.

"Where's the Colonel?" I asked when we had finished and were sitting by the fire down in the kitchen with a small beer in our pewter mugs.

"Gone to get a coffin made, then to the Parson to get a funeral made." Jonathan poured himself another beer. I went to my bag and pulled out a heavy fruited cake and cut chunks for each of us, they fell upon it as if they had never seen a sweet cake in their lives.

"Life here is not good?" I asked biting my cake.

"We mussen talk of it." Old Barry said with a mouthful of half chewed cake. "We' m lucky to have any work hereabouts."

"I will," Jonathan piped up, "I will talk of it, for I'm off to join the army and fight with the King on the Isle de Rhe." The room was filling with wood smoke from the fire and a couple of the candles had burnt down making the room cloudy and mysterious. "He made her a whore," he whispered to me.

"What?" I asked shocked, "God blind me, I had no idea. I work in his rooms in Oxford cleaning and cooking and running errands."

"Do 'ee pay ye?" Old Barry asked suddenly looking interested. She wiped her mouth on her petticoats and burped.

"No, I am one of the midwives of Oxford, I am paid well by my mothers and fathers. He gives me advice on what rises men, and what men are about. I cook and clean for him in return." I lied through my teeth, trying to equate the warm charming man I thought I knew, with the cold man who lived here and prostituted his young wife."

"So..." she laughed roughly, "you be his other missus."

"No, no," I flushed, "I am espoused to a man called Howard."

"Does he know that?" Jonathan looked at the cake, as I nodded to say he could take another chunk. The candles fluttered. This was a draughty old house.

"Never spoke of it." I stared into the crackling flames wondering who Artful really was, and hoping he would not come back that night.

"Well dun tell ' im Missus," Old Barry slumped in her chair by the fire, her face reddened with the beer and the heat, "dun tell ' im." She fell asleep worn out by her days labours, and started snoring. Jonathan had livened up as all young people do at night, his young eyes eagerly watching my face.

"She cut herself to let the pain out." He stared into his tankard. "That's what she do say to me. She takes the arsenic and quicksilver to stop her feeling."

I knew he was an innocent young lad. I knew from experience that the concoctions she had been taking were for the relief of the French pox. Then it became for her own relief and escape.

Jonathan was about fifteen or sixteen, but I could see he had lived more than his years by being in this household. He rubbed a rough hand over his face, brown from working in the fields. "Tis soldiering for me now, for the King, it's said he feeds well and pays well."

"Don't believe it, there's many a starving soldier in Oxford." I poked the fire, waking it up, sparks flew in the darkness, giving the shadows in the room a ghostly movement. Jonathan threw on a new log. "Is Old Barry your mother?" I asked.

"Lord no," He laughed, "Me come out of that?" He nodded to the snoring foetid lump.

"I'm told I'm a Lord's son, born the wrong side of the sheets, mother left me on the church step." He sighed, "Old Windybanks took me in."

It was a story I'd heard from many a young expectant mother, a roll in the hay with a young farm labourer, later in the telling, became the Lord of the Manor. People were less judgemental, as this sometimes did happen. They had more sympathy for the woman if she had been taken by a Lord, than if she had given herself freely to a farmhand – for that made her loose, a whore.

I got my cloak from my box, pulled it round my shoulders and drew nearer the fire. "Was she always a bawd? Did he take her from the streets?" I listened to Jonathan as he told me that Arthur had married a Miss Wilson, a pretty, dim witted, but innocent young girl. She was the daughter of a local landowner.

When he had gambled her dowry money away, and her father's after he had died. Alice Windybanks was to entertain his friends, the local gentry, for gold. But often the pillow talk was an added bonus. Artful had information he could sell. He became a spy.

I shuddered as I heard horse's hooves in the yard, Artful had arrived with the Rector and the Magistrate.

"Come, be quiet." Jonathan opened the wooden door beside the hearth to the servants staircase, he led me into a small dark corridor. We climbed the stairs and sat on them. Jonathan closed the door behind us. Soon we could hear voices echoing from the room above. We could hear quite clearly what was being said.

"Poisoned herself eh?" The Magistrate, Mr Button, clomped around the room in his bucket boots. "Damned waste, what say you Parson?"

I heard the Parson shuffle uncomfortably.

"Arsenic," Artful answered, "Got it from a wise woman, it was to help her sleep. God knows she got little enough rest when she was alive!" He laughed. He actually laughed. Sitting on the cold stone steps once again I heard my father's warning in my head. My father you were right, I am too trusting of men. No more. No more.

"Who laid her out?" Mr Button boomed, "Did a good job, looks like she did in her heyday."

"Brought a midwife from Oxford, knows her business, knows when keep her mouth shut," Artful laughed, "and hopefully her legs open."

I was about to speak when Jonathan's hand closed over my mouth. "Come." He whispered dragging me away.

"Where are we going?" I asked when we were back in the kitchen.

"To the Woodsman's hut, 'tis where I hide when I know he looks to beat me."

We crept through the damp darkness at the back of the house, taking my bags and the old horse. "Why am I hiding?" I asked.

"Do you want the fat old magistrate on top of you for gold tonight?" He asked as his eyes flickered around the dark trees.

"He wouldn't let that happen to me, I've known him for years." I whispered.

"Yes he would, now the poor missus is gone, God Bless her, how will he make his money?"

He opened the door to a bothy hidden under a pile of damp broken branches, we crawled in. I heard Arthur calling for me and was almost tempted to go, but Jonathan held me tight and put his hand over my mouth. We sat until we heard the horses gallop away into the distance.

"I'll go see if it's safe." He scuttled back to the house, then came back. When he stood in front of me he had tears in his eyes.

"What's amiss?" I watched his red rimmed eyes.

"I can't speak of it." He grabbed my arm and pulled me through the undergrowth, back to the house and up to Mrs Windybanks' room.

Old Barry was already at her mistresses' bedside sobbing heartily. "No rest." She mumbled drunkenly, "even when dead."

I couldn't believe my eyes. Alice's skirt and shift were pulled up to her waist and her gillyflower had been unpacked and used. There was a gold coin on the pillow beside her head.

I pulled her clothes straight. "Is the blacksmith hereabouts a good man?"

"Tis true." Jonathan stared at me.

"Take this." I gave him the gold coin, "Tell him to bring a horse and cart and take this poor woman to the nunnery. Tell them to put her in the chapel."

"The gold?" Jonathan looked scared, looking over his shoulder as if Artful would return at any minute.

"She earned it. It's for a decent burial and prayers said for her redemption."

We walked back to the bothy, lost in our own thoughts. I packed my bag over the tired old horse. "If he asks, tell him I commanded it."

The good thing about being a midwife is that you are used to being out and about at all hours of the day and night. But not usually alone. Susannah and my gossips were always round and about.

A birthing takes eight of us, Susannah and myself as midwives, and six women known as gossips. They kept an eye on us, and would make sure the child was not exchanged, or smothered at birth if it was healthy and strong. They looked after the mother's needs, talking to her, boiling water to bathe her and the child, changing the bedclothes, and telling her of all the news of the town to keep her distracted from the pain.

This morning, I had ridden in the darkness with the sun rising over the fields, on my own. Every moment with my heart in my mouth for the roads were full of thieves and mountebanks. I watched every dark shadow, every rabbit or owl, every rat that rustled in the hedgerow. Just outside Oxford I found I was on the road near St Andrew's churchyard in Sandford.

I met an honest farmer on his way to milk his cows with his milkmaids. They chattered and laughed in the half darkness. “Mornin' mistress midwife, who's been birthed this day?”

I waved a tired hand, “Been laying out, not bringing in.”

The farmer stopped in his tracks, “Plague is it? The small pox?” His tanned rugged face partially lit by the yellow sunlight of the upcoming day. He was worried, these diseases were never far from us.

“No, no,” I said sadly, “Just a lady who died in her sleep.” Which was partially true.

“A good age?” He asked as he moved on with his gaggle of milkmaids and churns.

“No, a young lady, a poor weak lady.” I answered as I spurred my gentle old horse on.

“God bless her and save her,” the gaggle of girls said almost together.

By the time my tired old horse found its way home and clip clopped into its familiar stable, the larks had been singing since the first light. I climbed the stairs to my room, exhausted. In an hour, the household would waken; pots of water would be boiled, bread would be taken from the oven cut and buttered, warm possets made, the tables set for breaking our fast.

I decided I could no longer be Artful's mistress or housekeeper. My mind felt full of must, so I tried to sleep, I had half a day on my former "love". I counted I had an hour to sleep, a half hour to break my fast. An hour to remonstrate with Susannah and her husband, an hour to clear Artful's rooms of the few things I kept there. Then to Howard and Charles my King, to perform my service to the crown. When Colonel Arthur Windybanks returned to his rooms, I would be long gone. He probably would not care, I was not a great beauty like his poor wife. I was just useful to him. That was all, I realised that now. I felt sorry for Jonathan and poor old Barry. I hoped he wouldn't beat them too badly.

It is said the best laid plans of mice, men and midwives go astray, and so mine did that day. It started with Susannah hammering on my door to wake me. "Dress niece, hurry, may I help?"

"No, no, I have nearly shifted all for myself, I'll be with you in a moment." I had actually fallen asleep in my clothes. I looked out of my window at the church clock, I had slept longer than the hour I had planned. All I needed to do was brush my hair under my coif and wash my hands and face. I straightened my petticoats and flicked rose water over them, checked myself in my mirror and ran downstairs in my hose, slipping on the wood. I had no time to put on or tie my shoes but I thought that as my skirts should cover my feet no-one would notice.

The faces that greeted me made me fall on my knees in shock.

"Mother, father, my Lord King." I watched my mother's face, lined, but still beautiful, although stern. My father picked me off the floor. He had not changed to me. Handsome with streaks of grey in his beard, age had improved him.

The King watched me recover myself. "Does my gift surprise you?" He smiled.

Aunt Susannah stood beside her sister, my mother, holding her hand. She was watching her face, smiling. They had not seen each other for over fourteen years.

I stared at them all smiling at me, all except mother. Had I at last, done something they could be proud of? "Mother." I dropped a curtsey in front of her, hoping for a touch of her hand or a smile. A near thirty year old, still feeling like the child of fifteen that she sent to Oxford in disgrace.

"Get up," she said angrily. "Where are your latchets?"

"Mother, I was told to hurry, so I did, I forgot myself." I bowed my head like a child. "I have been out this night laying out a young woman, a Lady, I am tired."

She sneered at me, turned her back on me as she walked towards the window to look out.

I felt a soft kid skin gloved hand on mine. "Look up my little one."

"Father," my eyes filled with tears, "I think of you every day, and the advice you gave me."

"What advice was that?" Mother asked spitefully, she spun round, her jealous eyes narrowing at me.

"Not to trust men." I looked into her cold blue eyes.

She walked across and linked her arm through fathers and looked up at him in the most warm, loving way. I had never seen her look at me like that.

"Well, well, family Farthing, w..what do we think?" The King spoke, I had almost forgotten he was there.

"She may marry Lord Howard if you deem it Your Majesty." My father smiled at me, "Do you wish it, my child?"

"Tis a waste of time, she is past the bloom of youth, there will be no children to speak of." Mother snapped nastily.

"But there will be love." Howard smiled as he walked into the room towards me and put his arm out for me, for mine to rest upon. I smiled up at him. Speechless for once.

Mother smiled scornfully at me. Being a midwife, I now understood why Mother hated me so. I was the first born, taken immediately to a wet nurse. She did not feel the ribbons of love form as I call them. The ribbons form when a baby is first given to the mother, she will smile, kiss its little head, gently stroking it's skin. She will smell its forehead, it will smell of the wash we have given it, a new baby smelling of rosewater or vanilla. Then it is put to the breast, and the mother smiles as the child suckles. Proud of her little one, her precious achievement.

But take the child away immediately, as is done for all the best people in all the Castles and Manors of the land, and the ribbons of love do not form as they should. Sometimes the child is rejected, as I was. Sometimes love will grow over time as it did with my brother. I know little of my mother's childbearing life, but I know she can't love me, the ribbons are torn to pieces. They cannot be mended. I have seen it happen too often.

Woodstock, June 1645

I have taken to writing a diary. Years have passed. Mostly not unkindly to me. I live just outside Woodstock in a pretty Manor Farm, untouched by the Civil War which has been burning a scar across my beloved England for three years now.

Much has changed, we have all aged, the King is 45 years old and I am 49 years old. I have been Lady Howard for a goodly while. I love my husband as much as I did when we married, but my love has not grown as much or as deeply as the King's love for his pretty French wife Henrietta. They have become the loving parents of nine children, eight of whom live.

The spying that dear King Charles engaged me for, turned out to be nothing more than listening to the gossip of the Court. I was to report to him anything I thought of interest. It was no more exciting than being a tell-tale tit. However, I had to be Lady Howard to do it.

As for Artful, he disappeared from Oxford society soon after I left. I no longer cared or wanted to know what he was about.

I am indeed now Lady Howard. I have one daughter, named Katherine, for my mother. I suppose I am happy enough in my life, but I am lonely.

I know now that my Lord has always preferred young men to me. He says constantly that he loves me. Strangely, I know that he does love me truly. For the past twenty years we have been happy loving companions, shared confidences and a bed but he does not make love to me. Even though decreed by the church that he should. However, the clergy are not in every bedroom in the land.

When you are younger you do not think of consequences. I did not think at all in St. Giles Church when my King offered me my Lord Howard for a husband what the consequences would be. I did not realise the cost to his first wife. It was her family that provided the Manor in which I now live, the farm that provides our living, the money I spend on provender and clothing is her money. It is also her money that pays for my Lord's increasing gambling debts.

Women are but property. She was cast out, back to her family, blamed for the non consummation of the marriage, left without her dowry and her home. Everything she had owned now belonged to him, and by default to me. Sometimes living in Stonesfield Manor makes me feel like a thief.

In the first years I was blissfully ignorant and happy in my love for him. Kept myself so, making a busy life with my growing little girl and my household.

Howard and I were close friends, confiding in each other. Lying in bed together at night forehead to forehead, laughing at the world and it's ups and downs. We both loved our daughter dearly, I hoped a son would follow.

Quite often, the melancholy black dog would return to sit with my Lord and he would shut himself away and sob. I made the medicines that helped him when he was a student in Oxford, but they no longer worked. A deep darkness lived in him some days, and even I couldn't reach through it.

The only thing that seemed to help was hunting, it lifted his spirits, he would come back happy and refreshed. Then life would continue as usual for a little while at least.

What I did not know was that the hunting took place not in the lush green fields and forests of our land. It took place in the smoky, ribald, gaming rooms and bawdy houses of Oxford. Full of young men dressed and painted as women. It was his way of coming to terms with living a lie. He loved me as a friend, as a sister, not a wife. He could not in all faith take me as his wife. I often thought how true the old Gypsy woman's predictions had become, I had indeed been crossed by two men. I wish she had predicted more happiness for me. Like the happiness I felt when I danced at the Bear Inn with Artful for the first time. Like the happiness Susannah and Thomas had cultivated between themselves over the years of their marriage.

I had felt young and happy once. It seemed so many years ago now. It was many years ago. I now feel my time is up as I go about my business in the Manor and the Farm. I have no energy. It seems the time my Lord spends with me is getting less and less, everyone is consumed with the war. My Lord Howard is passionately involved with his support of the King. I'm sure it will not be long before he takes our small regiment to the battlefield in his defence.

When I was a child and lived at the Palace with mother and father, I would hear the maids and footmen gossip about the old King James. They laughed in corners of the kitchen where they couldn't be heard talking treason.

The old King liked pretty young men, chose a few as his favourites. When he had masques and balls, many of them would dress as women. Except the Duke of Buckingham, he was so outstandingly beautiful as a man, no women's dress could improve him. His finely turned calves were clothed in white hose embroidered with gold silk around his ankles. He wore his long golden hair, curled. It luxuriantly tumbled over the expensive gold embroidered doublet studded with pearls bought for him by the King. He strutted through the palace like a peacock, but woe betide anyone who caught the sharp side of his waspish tongue. The smelly old King would watch his court, smiling, his hand constantly inside his breeches touching and re-arranging his privates. As a child I didn't understand what it meant. But there came a day soon after marrying Howard, when the crowns fell into my purse and I knew it all.

We have had many little adventures together during this cursed war. The only thing we did not share was each other's bodies, apart from the wedding night, nine months after which, my daughter was born. There have been kisses and caresses and we hold each other while we sleep. "Like the babes in the wood." Howard smiled one evening. "We are like a loving brother and sister."

"Why are we not like loving husband and wife?" I asked with tears in my eyes.

"You can blame that on my parents." Howard stroked my hair from my eyes. "It was when I was on the Grand Tour that I was introduced to what my true nature was. Had I not experimented with the Italian ways, I may have been a true husband yet."

"Howard, this is not fair, I am true to you, yet you are not true to me." I sobbed.

"It is for your safety my dear, it's because I love you. I may have something that I should not wish you to catch." He held me close. "Be happy little one, my dear one."

"But my love, I have devices that may stop that happening." I pleaded.

"Sweet Anne, it is my vices that you cannot stop. Be content my love." He smiled stroking my hair. "We have each other."

That was the end of it.

I have many silk dresses, a large house, footmen, housekeepers, cooks and skivvies, and I write. What a scandal it is to write, but my dear husband not only allows it, but encourages me. I write a secret diary that I hide in my closet. I write books for young women like my daughter, to help them run their households. I have included good posset recipes, even expensive ones that include the new found coffee. I tell them how to please their husbands, for a man content at home will not wander. Believe that if you may.

I have been faithful, loving and true to my Howard, keeping up my side of our bargain. He has provided me with the very best in life, except himself. Sometimes I cry into my hands and wonder if having almost everything is enough?

It's hot for June. My husband left to join the King a day ago. A messenger has just arrived to tell me that my Lord Howard is already at Naseby. Sitting on his beautiful roan horse on the steep Northamptonshire hill beside Charles and Rupert no doubt.

"Mother." A pretty light voice breaks me from my thoughts.

"Yes sweet one." I look up at my daughter, tall and fair like her father.

Today she is dressed in a pale blue silk dress with a stomacher of dark blue embroidered with pearls. Her hair is curled around her ears and bobs when she moves. I cannot believe I have made such a beautiful creature from my own body.

"I may have need of your services at last." She grinned brightly, sweeping across the room to me. She has been married to, in my opinion, a feckless youth two years her junior, for eighteen months now. Her own choice, and surprisingly her father approved of it. The son of a minor aristocrat, wealthy enough, lazy enough, he hunted, and gamed, but not too much. He was rather aimlessly trying to learn the life of a country squire so that he and Katherine could leave our Manor for a smaller one of their own given by his father.

"Where is Richard today?" I asked, wondering what his latest idea was. He was a young man who took up and dropped any ideas that he had decided to follow, as quickly as he'd thought of them.

"At Naseby of course, with father and the King." She swirled around humming a tune. "Mother, I am so happy." She stopped in front of a mirror, pulling the curls on her forehead towards her prettily arched brows, painted on that very morning.

"Long may it last." I suddenly realised I sounded like my own mother and bit my tongue.

"What do you mean?" Her lovely clear green eyes watched my face.

"The war," I stood up from my desk and walked across to the window where she was standing, "we may be widows yet."

"Mother, really, you say the strangest things." She smiled and swirled to the door. "I love to feel my pearls bounce on my skin." She nodded her head from side to side and her pearl earrings hit her cheeks gently and smoothly. "Lovely is it not?" Katherine closed the door as she left.

"So I say the strangest things?" I smiled going back to my desk and closing my writing book.

The door opened and our footman, Carpenter, popped his head round. "Lady, there is a man who claims acquaintance with you waiting in the hallway. He seems a rough sort, what shall I do?"

My mind was racing, was it Artful after all these years? I felt hot and sick. "Tell him to go into the long gallery, send my maid along with some lemon and rose water. Tell him you will have to find me, tell him I will be along shortly." I walked up the back stairs by the kitchen to look at my visitor from the minstrel's gallery. It wasn't Artful, this was a vibrant young man with long black curling hair, he was too short to be my brother. He was dressed as an Officer of the Royalist Horse, he was wearing a red sash over his old yellow buff coat and a black felt hat with red and white ostrich feathers. He took his gloves off to drink his lemon water as he walked about the room looking at the portraits on the walls.

He sat on a chair opposite the minstrel's gallery, but I still couldn't see his face, hidden by his black felt hat. Under his well worn bucket boots, I saw a flash of yellow hose. So he was a young unmarried man.

Years ago, as an unmarried woman living with my aunt Susannah, I liked men. I liked the smell of wood smoke in their hair, the strength of their hands when they put them around my waist when we went to dance as they lifted me up to the tune. To me, at that time, there was nothing better than a well turned male calf in a yellow hose. Yellow means he is available, unmarried, therefore prey! That was how I met Arthur, at a dance at one of the taverns in Oxford, so very long ago now. He was introduced to me as a good friend of Susannah's husband who was a kind man, a good man. I believed Artful to be the same. Although I must have felt something amiss, because I started calling him Artful, almost immediately.

I clattered downstairs to see the visitor.

He bowed low, sweeping his flamboyant felt hat off his head as he did so.

"Is my husband dead? Is Richard Boyons dead?" I snapped without thinking.

The young man laughed and it echoed through the gallery. "You do not know your old friend and saviour?" He stood up, dark eyes flashed in an intelligent face, "It was over twenty years ago in an old bothy that we last spoke."

"God's teeth, Jonathan!" I hugged him tightly to me then I released the poor breathless lad. "Is it really you?" I pulled him by the hand to my parlour, "I have so much to ask you."

As I dragged him along, asking questions, I called to Carpenter to bring some beer.

"Are you hungry?" I asked sitting him down. "Carpenter, bring this young officer some provender, the best we have, capon, bread, cheese, a salat."

"Madam, madam, calm yourself, I am no longer a starving waif!" He grinned, his teeth were good and clean.

I sat opposite him trying to take it all in. This was Artful's farm hand, footman, child slave. Now he was a Royalist Officer, with a handsome face, a curling waxed moustache and small beard on his chin in the latest style.

"You have grown so, I did not know you." I laughed stroking his cheek, "look at you."

"You have grown more beautiful madam, more courtly, yet I shall always know you." His eyes softened. "I am on my way to Naseby, I heard you lived on my way, so bethought it time to reacquaint myself."

"When do you leave to join the King?" I asked smiling, "Not too soon before we catch up?"

"I am one of Prince Rupert's Bluecoats." He grinned as the food arrived. "What no cake?"

"Ask Ruth for some fruit cake, Carpenter. This officer has need of great sustenance." Carpenter rolled his eyes at me as if it were a great problem, but went off to do as he was bid nonetheless.

"So?" I asked pouring him a beer, "What news?"

Before he could speak, in a cloud of expensive perfume and fine silk, my daughter appeared in the doorway. Jonathan stood and bowed low. Katherine smiled blindingly at him, she had changed into a cream day dress with dark underskirts.

"Jonathan, this is my daughter Katherine." I held my hand out to her.

"Unbelievable. You are too young to be this lady's mother," he smiled. I looked at my darling girl, and the realisation for her change of clothes dawned on me. Her courses had started after two months, she was not pregnant after all. She didn't seem displeased, but that was my Katherine, whatever happened was no problem to her. She was just like her father in that respect. She sat beside me and I squeezed her hand, we did not need to speak of it, she knew immediately what I meant.

Carpenter brought the fruit cake in and Katherine made a grab for it laughing. "She puts porter in the cake, that's why it's so delicious. I can't stop eating it once it's made."

"Leave some for Jonathan." I smiled passing the best pewter platters round. I felt two things I hadn't felt before towards my daughter. One was annoyance, I wanted to catch up with Jonathan and find out what happened to Artful, in private. The other was jealousy, Katherine had perfect creamy skin without a blemish, big bright green eyes, a trim waist, and was young. Jonathan couldn't stop looking at her which was unsurprising, but suddenly I wanted to be young and pretty again and have the attention of this young man.

"When are you to leave?" I asked, "Can you stay tonight so we may catch up?"

"Lady Anne," he smiled at me making me feel a hundred years old. "Of course, the battle is the day after tomorrow, it will take me a day to ride from Woodstock to Naseby. I would be pleased to take my rest here tonight."

"Well, I cannot stay," Katherine pouted, "Richard's parents are expecting me to dinner tonight, so I will stay with them." She stood up snatching another piece of cake, "I swear mother this will be only decent food I will have till I come back to your household." She turned to Jonathan, "Do NOT discuss anything juicy or interesting until I get back."

I laughed, "My darling do not worry yourself on that account, I will tell you all when you get home."

She swished out to tell the Boyons that she was not pregnant after all, and watch their disappointed faces as they realised that their son had once more failed in his duty to provide them with an heir.

In my kitchens Ruth and Carpenter were talking about my guest.

"Calls himself an officer, so he does." Carpenter took some small beer and a hunk of bread. Ruth cut him some cheese and a hunk of cake, he put it on his trencher. "Is there any meat?"

"A bit of capon," Ruth broke the wings off with a bit of the breast and scraped some salt onto the bird. "Enough?" She smiled. She didn't really like Carpenter, but she kept him on side. The Irish were difficult people to handle she thought, he was either moaning or drunk or both. She locked her door every night, but he didn't seem bothered about that kind of thing, but she felt safer doing it.

"He's up to something, mark my words," he took a swig of beer. Ruth made herself a posset from my recipe book to see if it worked. It was part of her job. So she made the most expensive posset containing coffee, cream and wine. She smiled, this recipe was very nice indeed. "Perhaps he's not, perhaps he's just a messenger."

"Could be, could be." Carpenter bit the cold meat. "Done well with this girl. Thank ee. I'm never too big to say thank ee when it's due."

"Will you go fight in the war?" Ruth's plain little face watched Carpenter's hooded eyelids flicker as he thought about it. "I won't need to maid, the war will come to us, mark my words."

There was only Carpenter and Ruth left in the house to serve the Howards, not by cowardice but from loyalty. Most of the men were in who were in our little company had left with Lord Howard. Ruth had lost her elder brother to his enthusiasm to join the war. She had no will to see it at first hand like our skivvy Maggie, who had left to join the baggage train in search of more excitement than scrubbing pots.

Ruth gave a little shudder. It would soon be time to lock the windows and doors, how could their wooden shutters keep out soldiers? She sipped her posset and tried not to think about it.

It was a warm balmy night and I took Jonathan out onto the terrace. I showed him our land, the smoke from the cooking fires of the little town of Woodstock drifted from the chimneys into the warm air above the cottages.

"You never married?" I asked watching his handsome face in the fading daylight.

"No, I was waiting for you." He smiled half jokingly. "Are you happy?"

"I don't know." I answered, "I should be, but I'm not. I feel each day is worthless and I am just waiting to die. Tis only my dear daughter that I live for, and when she leaves, my job is done and my life is over."

Jonathan looked shocked and took my hand. "What you consider is a mortal sin, Hell forever. Your life is not like that of Mrs Windybanks'."

"No." I considered our joint horror that night in Little Coxwell Manor. How hurt and scared the young Jonathan was.

"What about Lord Howard?" He asked holding my hand, "What think you of him?"

"You are in Rupert's, as is my husband, you must know as well as I do that it is not a woman's love that moves him. I fared better than his first wife, he could not touch her at all," I sighed. "Our wedding night was normal enough, he had trouble, but I thought it was all his friends hammering and singing outside the door that put him off, but he managed to do the deed. It was the one and only time he did." I felt tears run down my face, "from that night I have my beautiful girl. Named for my mother, for I thought it would make her love me."

"Did it?" He asked.

"No." I turned away from him to watch the darkness fall like a black velvet cloak over the land.

He took my arm and gently stroked it as we walked back towards the house. He told me that Colonel Windybanks had helped incense a young officer called Tom Felton to kill the Duke of Buckingham. When Artful heard from local gossips that the Duke had cut my skirts with his sword in St. Giles, he assumed that he'd ravished me. He took that to be the reason why the King had married me off so quickly to Lord Howard.

I smiled in the darkness, the tears ran salty into my mouth, such a mix of feelings. “Where is Artful now?” I looked into Jonathan's handsome face.

“He has become a buccaneer, and loves the life,” he grinned, “it suits him.” He caught my arm again. “You're shivering my lady, let us go into the house.”

The Manor, over warm during the day, was now chilly. Ruth was lighting the fire in my drawing room, she lit two candlesticks on the mantel and left a burning taper on one so I could light more if I wished. I heard her and Carpenter's footsteps as they hurried round the house, locking the doors and shuttering the windows.

We sat together beside the fire. I was starting to warm up so I untied the lace collar from my neck.

“You are so beautiful,” Jonathan's finger gently traced along my chin and down the curve of my neck to my shoulder where it lingered.

“You are too kind.” I smiled at him, “but you know what they say, never choose a woman or a dog by candlelight.”

He took off his jacket, put it on the floor by the fire, and lay on it. He guided me from my chair to sit with him.

“Remember that night in the Bothy? We sat scared for what seemed hours in the cold.”

I smiled at him, he had a look I recognised but had not seen for nearly twenty years. He was almost in a dream like state as his soft fingers traced along the lace of my bodice and the skin of my bosoms.

“How old are you?” I asked, taking his exploring fingers out of the top of my bodice.

“Thirty five.” He smiled undoing the laces that held my bodice together. He pulled them undone more quickly than I have ever seen any man do, using only his two thumbs. My shift, soft and white, clung to my breasts from being pressed close under my gown during the heat of the day.

“I'm nearly fifty.” I smiled sadly, not stopping him, “My time is nearly done.”

"Never." He pulled me close to him and kissed me full on the mouth. "I remembered your kindness as I travelled through the world." His hands slid underneath my shift, up my smooth cold thighs. "I remembered you looking back at me."

I couldn't deny it, but where a fifteen year old boy saw love, perhaps even lust. I saw a fifteen year old boy that I was worried to leave with a violent man.

He moved against me until his rhythm matched my breathing. "I tried to find you." He whispered as he took me, "No-one would tell me where you were."

I couldn't speak, after so many years the pleasure was intense, to be wanted, perhaps even loved again. "So I'm going to hell whatever I do!" I whispered as I arched my back to accommodate him.

"Well, I'm coming with you then." He smiled, as he kissed me hard on the lips.

At the Boyons' farmhouse, Katherine was trying to explain to Richard's mother in the small parlour, that again there would be no heir this month.

"It's your fault girl, you're obviously barren." She pinched Katherine's arms, "Look at you – all skin and bones, there's nothing of you."

My daughter pulled away roughly, "Madam I am not a beast to be so poked and prodded."

Lady Boyons' slit of a mouth curled downwards. She had mean little eyes that flickered over Katherine's fine dress. "It's all for fashion with you. I suppose you eat gruel like the queen to keep so slim."

Katherine was about to say that actually she could eat whatever she liked and keep her figure, she was active, rode, danced and walked and what not. But as she opened her mouth to speak her mother in law hissed one word. "Tace."

She looked at Lady Boyons, but she saw fright in her face – not anger. So that was why she'd spoken so harshly to her daughter in law to be silent. There was a rustling outside the house, the geese were screaming in the yard. There was the sound of marching feet coming closer, they could hear horses snorting and whinnying.

Lady Boyons pulled Katherine to her closet which was hidden behind a tapestry, shutting the door and locking it from the inside.

"Where are the men of the household ?" A strong man's voice with a London accent asked.

"Master is with his horses," their old servant answered, " 'tis just he and me tonight."

"No women?" The Puritan Colonel strode about the room, picking up this and that ornament and putting it back in the wrong place.

"Just the cook. My wife." The old man stuttered, "She's not well Sir, she has the ague."

"Ague or not, we are being billeted here tonight. The officers will take the house and the soldiers may take the stables and the fields hereabouts. Get the cook to bring forth food and wine." The officer put his white kid gloves on the finely polished table beside his hat and sword. "We go to fight the good fight at Cropredy tomorrow, then forwards to Naseby field."

Katherine's first instinct was to run out and shout, "How dare you take over my mother's house?" But Lady Boyons, older, wiser and meaner, held her tight.

She put her hand over her mouth and whispered in her ear. "This is my closet, I keep a sleeping draught locked in the corner cupboard here, perhaps we can get some into that Roundhead's wine." She took a small green medicine bottle from the shelf.

"How will we do that?" Katherine whispered.

"Ways and means." Lady Boyons' mean slit of a mouth turned up at the edges, she pulled a cord by the small fireplace in the room.

"What was that? Was that a bell?" The Colonel stood up and put his hand on his sword.

"No sir, just the wind, it takes the bell ropes sometimes, tis a pain." The old man put the wine and the glass on the table "Tis behind the tapestry – shall I tie it off? I generally does it overnight to quieten the house."

The Colonel nodded, and the old man put his hand behind the tapestry. Her Ladyship slipped the small green bottle into his sleeve.

The door burst open, "Colonel Birch." The Colonel turned to see the red coat of a New Model Army sergeant at the door. "There is good provender here, geese, hens, sheep, coneys, beer and Rhenish wine. What say you?"

"Take all but two of everything, so like Noah and the Ark, they may rebuild." He smiled, "I have a fancy for a good pie, if you see such in the kitchen bring it forth."

"The men, sir, need full bellies to fight." The soldier's raddled face smiled, his dark eyebrows lifted as if in a question. "What say you?"

"Have they prayed to God this night?" Colonel Birch poured himself some wine and slumped in a comfortable chair by the fire.

"They have sir, they have." He smiled a broken toothed grin.

"Then it's God's bounty – take all from these miscreants – eat, drink, make a joyful noise unto the Lord, for tomorrow we set off to win the day." Colonel Birch put his foot on the heel of his boot and pushed it off, the soldier bent forward to help with the other boot.

"Yes sir, thank 'ee sir."

"What are we to do?" Katherine whispered watching Lady Boyons' round face, pale in the darkness.

"Keep alive." She snapped quietly, "They will be gone tomorrow and we can live."

"Without food, without stock?" Her daughter in law looked puzzled.

"All can be bought again." Lady Boyons took a rug from the linen box, covered herself with it and sat in one of the chairs. "Come lady, be strong. Do not let me sleep for I snore and we will be found out."

"How can you sleep?" Katherine sat on the floor to see if she could hear anything.

All she heard were rowdy male voices singing.

'Teach me, my God and King, In all things Thee to see,

And what I do in anything To do it as for Thee.

A man that looks on glass, On it may stay his eye;

Or if he pleaseth, through it pass, And then the heaven espy.'

I don't understand, she thought, these are men of God. How could they steal and not think it was wrong? Didn't they believe in the ten commandments? Thou shalt not steal is the seventh commandment, I know that, and I'm not a quick study. She looked through the keyhole of the closet, but could only see the back of the tapestry.

"Katherine," Lady Boyons hissed, "Sit down, they will hear you."

"Mother, I must get home to my own mother, she is on her own tonight." She whispered back.

"She will be safe enough, if they are quartered here, they have no need to go further back again." Lady Boyons grabbed Katherine's arm and dug her nails in, "For Gods sake child, you'll give us away." She whispered harshly.

Old Godfrey came back with a pie for the Colonel. "Tis rabbit pie, all that's left, the missus put some bread and pickle with it." His hands shook as he put the meal on the table, the Colonel noticed it immediately. "Have you eaten this eve?"

"I dun eat too much, my teeth do hurt me sire." Godfrey stood shaking, " I'm sore afraid, you look to be good men, sound men. We are poor folk, I beg you sir, leave us peaceful."

"Take this bread and bite it, and this pie," Colonel Birch cut a small piece of pie and handed it to the old man who bit it with his back teeth and swallowed it. He took a slice of the the bread and sucked it.

"Good man." Colonel Birch laughed, now convinced the food was not poisoned. He tucked into the meal, and washed it down with the laudanum loaded Rhenish wine. The Colonel was soon in a heavy sleep.

"What now?" Katherine asked as the closet door was opened by Godfrey.

"Food and drink, enough for a couple of days," Lady Boyons smiled, "To keep us until we provide for ourselves again. We stay here till the morn and the Roundheads are gone."

Godfrey rolled a barrel of beer and pulled a sack of flour into the closet. Quickly followed by a sugar loaf, such herbs and spices as could be grabbed quickly, a couple of fresh dead hens and a rabbit. "Tes all I could carry." Godfrey's wiry arms pushed the provender into the small closet.

"Good enough Godfrey, get your Lizzie out if you can, bring her here," Lady Boyons gave a thin smile. "Then can you get word to my husband?"

Godfrey didn't answer, he just quivered and sucked his lips.

"What mean you?" She asked. "Tell me man, quickly?"

"You'm find out tomorrow my lady." He pushed her back into the closet.

"I'm leaving." Katherine pushed past the old man, "I can't stay here."

"No," Godfrey's bony hands clutched at her arm. "Tes not safe."

"I must go to my mother." Katherine picked up her skirts and sidled past Colonel Birch snoring into his dinner. She tiptoed across the room, worried he would hear her silk rustle and wake up.

"Let her go." Lady Boyons snapped, "Come in here Godfrey, there's no need for you to die as well."

Katherine didn't hear what her mother in law said as she was creeping along the unlit kitchen corridor. The London Trayned bands were clattering pots and pans, stealing as much food as they could carry in their snapsacks. Outside she could hear the strangled cries of livestock being killed.

In the pitch darkness she slid into the yard and kicked against something soft. Old Lord Boyons lay in a pool of blood at her feet. Katherine retched but put her hand over her mouth. She had to tread on his back to get out of the door, her heart pumping fit to burst she trod on the old man. Soon she was in the yard heading for the stables.

Most of the soldiers were sitting round their cooking fires, their tents had been put up in the neighbouring field where the geese had lived. Their camp strung down the hill towards the river. The acrid smell of wood smoke filled the air. They laughed loudly at each other's ribald jokes occasionally stopping to sing a snatch of a hymn.

She turned towards the stables looking behind her and walked in the pitch blackness straight into a soldier pissing against the wall. He was in mid stream and didn't really see who had knocked into him, what he did see was the flash of cream silk in the darkness disappearing through the stable doors. He quickly followed as soon as his flow allowed. Katherine was hiding behind her horse.

"Come out strumpet." He shouted making the horses skittish and kick the stable doors, "I know you're in here."

She didn't move.

"Come on, I won't harm 'ee lady, I'm a kind man." He laughed and snorted, filling Katherine with disgust. She heard him spit his snot on the floor of the stables.

Her horse raised her head and sneezed in her owner's face, Katherine couldn't help but gasp.

"Gotcha." She had recognised the man's voice, it was Colonel Birch's sergeant, his brown raddled, pock marked face was soon staring into hers. "Pretty little thing," he sneered pulling her from behind her chestnut mare who kicked and struggled on her reins.

He lit a lantern that had fallen over and was lying on the floor near the door. "Lets get a look at cha."

The sergeant was a man who could have been thirty or forty, he had seen action, he had sword scars on his face. Stringy but strong in build, he walked round Katherine giving a slow whistle. "Tasty." She kept turning to face him as he walked round her.

"Take off your gown." He growled licking his lips, "Gown off now."

"No." Katherine's voice was quiet but firm.

"Be a good girl and take it off and I won't call me mates." He grinned at her as he pushed her against the wall. Face to face, his breath smelt of shit. She struggled free. "Why should I take it off? If you want me you only have to lift my skirts, mister holy puritan soldier." She spat sarcastically.

He laughed, "It's the silk, stupid cow, I want to sell it, it's worth a fortune." He grabbed her and cut the laces of her gown with his dagger, as he pulled the gown off her shoulders, she struggled, but wasn't strong enough. The glittering cream gown fell into the hay at her feet. "Step out of it, there's a good girl." He rushed to the gown, rolled it up quickly and hid it in his bedroll.

"Good job I was guarding the horses this night. God is good to the brave." He moved towards Katherine shivering in her shift behind her mare. "Now." He smiled brokenly at her.

"You belong to the Devil not God." Katherine was angry and adrenalin was rising in her. "Nor are you brave, fighting an unarmed woman."

The sergeant ignored her and pulled her out of the stables into the light of the lantern.

He moved behind her, one arm across her throat, his other hand pinching her soft breasts painfully. He leant against her to bite her neck but Katherine bit him hard on the cheek drawing blood and struggled violently to free herself from his iron like grip.

"I'm not fussy, I'll have you alive or dead." His rancid breath was on her cheek making her want to vomit from the smell.

He pulled her head back onto his shoulder, her beautiful green eyes turned away from his raddled brown face. He stroked her neck with the cold steel of his dagger snagging on her clean white skin. She could hear her heart beating loudly in her ears as he gently traced her throat with the blade. "There's another reason why you had to take if off mistress. I do find, it's harder to sell a gown that's soaked in blood."

Stonesfield Manor, 14th June 1645

The soft grey light of a cloudy morning started to filter through the heavy tapestry curtains of the bedroom. I traced my finger down the cheek of the handsome young man in my bed. He didn't wake, he sighed as a smile fleetingly crossed his lips. I knew the ways of men. He had been fed, wined and entertained. It was all a man could ask for before going into battle. I would never see him again, it had been pleasant enough for me. I felt young, beautiful again, the years had dropped from me with each thrust of his hips.

I watched the fine clouds of spider's webs shine like silver as they caught the early morning sun under my wooden dresser. I slid out between the linen sheets to use the piss pot. It was in my personal closet behind the door in the corner of my bedroom, so I was able relieve myself for a goodly while in private. There are some things a man should never see a woman do, however much he professes to love her.

I washed my hands and face in the bowl on the little table. My face in the mirror was ghostly in the half light, I was a spectre of a woman. On the wall beside the jug and bowl hung the white bone cross my husband had bought for me on our honeymoon. I shuddered involuntarily, surely God will punish me for this.

Fingers of bright light were pushing their way through the heavy tapestry curtains as the house started to come to life. Pots clattered in the kitchen and the cockerel crowed loudly again and again in the yard. The fragrance of freshly baked bread rose up the stairwell. I looked from the closet window across the muddy yard at the back of the house. Fog was forming on the hills in the distance, it looked like it was going to be a warm muggy day.

I went to the press pulled out a clean shift and put it on. I laced my bodies together at the front and quickly pulled on a day dress of light linen. So dressed, I woke my Cavalier.

"Time to wake." I shook his shoulder, he turned, his long dark hair partly across his face. He looked so young, so beautiful. His strong bare chest was covered with sword scars that I had not noticed before in the darkness. When his bright brown eyes opened, my heart jumped with pleasure.

He smiled at me."Bless me madam, if I die today, I die a happy man." He picked up my hand, held it to his lips and kissed it. "You are a true beauty."

"You sir, are too young for me." I smiled, "But I forgive you for it, as you are mature enough to know better."

I could hear Ruth coming up the stairs. "Jakes in the closet and water to wash. Quickly!"

I admired his lithe muscular body as he rushed past me pulling his clothes into to the small dressing room.

As my servant girl Ruth entered, I kicked his bucket boots under the bed out of her sight.

"Madam, would you break your fast in the kitchen or dining room today?" She smiled watching me trying to hide my lovers boots with my heel.

"Kitchen Ruth." I frowned at her.

"Madam." She started, her plain little face a picture of puzzlement.

"Say nothing to me, say nothing about me." I pushed her out of the door and leant on it.

I could hear her laughing on the stairs.

"So, the old maid was on heat." Carpenter laughed as Ruth and he talked together. They bustled round as they laid the table. "I wish I had known, I'd have quenched her thirst." He thrust a wooden rolling pin into the air with a suggestive pushing motion. "Aye, I'd have shown her what was what!" He grimaced.

In a second, Carpenter was swearing in Irish. Jonathan had punched him on the side of his head with some force. "Do NOT speak of your mistress in such terms man. I would call you out but I have a battle to fight today."

"What in God's name is going on?" I came in to sit at the top of the table. I watched the reddened faces around me. "Is mistress Katherine returned?"

Both the heavily bruised Carpenter, and my little maid Ruth uttered an almost silent "No."

Jonathan had an appetite which made us all gasp. He took bread with butter, even though he was not sick. Gobbets of bacon, a bowl of porridge, and quenched his thirst with a small beer with honey. "I may not see this day out, so as this is my last meal I wish to enjoy as much as I can eat, have you cheese and apples?"

"Sur, the apples not be that ripe, they be sharp." Carpenter gave him a red apple and slice of cheese.

Jonathan cut the apple to put a piece of cheese on it.

"Will do." he smiled as he tasted the two together. He started wrapping his leftovers in a piece of linen and put them into his snapsack.

I walked with him to the stable yard as Carpenter, complaining as usual, went off to saddle and fetch Jonathan's horse.

"Will I ever see you again?" I asked as I leant on his arm.

He smiled at me, "It depends what this day brings."

"Be careful." I whispered to him.

"Do you have a message for Lord Howard?" He asked, "Shall I tell him not to come home as all his affairs have been taken care of?" He grinned broadly.

I gave him a playful punch on the shoulder.

"Oh now I cannot fight for I am wounded." He joked as he leapt on to his horse's back.

"How Sir, are you wounded?" I laughed.

"I have an arrow through my heart." He smiled pulling his horse up to rear dramatically on it's back legs, then turned, and in a moment they were gone through the mist.

Carpenter make a disgusted clucking sound as he turned back to the house rubbing his sore ear. He was determined to tell his master he had been cuckolded as soon as he stepped over the threshold.

I had been sorting through my herbs and potions, though my days of being a midwife were long over, my household were still in need of care. I had lotions for sore dry hands; tansy water for taking away the smell of sweaty feet; dried mint, sage and lavender to kill bad humours and clean wounds; rosewater, honey and tallow to make soap.

The heady fragrances of the herbs took me back to Theobalds Palace where the Royal Gardener, John Tradescant, was brought to build the herb gardens there. He had been newly married and often brought his baby son with him in his wheelbarrow to sit and watch as he worked. As a young girl I would stand by watching him working, asking him questions as I occasionally played with the child.

"What herb is this sir?" I picked up some fragrant leaves and teased the baby with them.

"Savoury, so called as 'tis good for flavouring the stews." He snatched it from me and put it into the earth. His hands were hardened and calloused, but for all that, gentle and firm around the plant roots.

"Why dost thou bring baby John? Has he no mother?" I asked swirling round on the grass.

Baby John laughed as he tried to grab my dress.

"I am to go away, I won't see my son for many a year." He stood up and stretched his back. "I may not see him ever again, who knows what the future brings?"

"Why are you to go away?" I asked looking at the herbs that were waiting to be planted. They were laid neatly on the lawn, their roots wrapped in damp linen to keep them fresh.

"Why do you ask so many questions girl?" John picked up his son and swung him up onto his broad shoulders, the boy giggled. "Your parents are the teachers not I." He walked towards the house to get water from the pump.

"They teach the Royal children. Not me, they have no time for me." I tagged after him.

"Then they are fools," he snapped gruffly.

As I rushed away from him back into the garden through the lavender hedges, butterflies and bees burst from the flowers as I ran and skipped through the bushes. They made a colourful confetti of living things for me to run through, my dark hair was untied and I had pushed daisies into it.

John stared over at me playing in his garden. "How could they not love you, so full of life as you are?" He muttered as he chucked his son under his chin, he stared into his brown eyes. "My son, I will love you truly, and will care for you and your family as long as I live, I will teach you my secrets to make gardens grow, and you will find richness in life, this I swear." John Tradescant said nothing else for the rest of the day. While his son slept in the hay in the wheelbarrow, he worked steadily until the light failed then he covered the child with his doublet and wheeled him home to his wife.

I walked towards the palace with some roses and lavender as a present for my mother. Perhaps she would love me if I gave her flowers. She did not love me for bringing her flowers, she beat me with a cane for stealing from the King's garden.

The memories burnt me, the smell of the herbs brought it all back. I could not get melancholic, there was much to do. A war on our doorstep could mean I would need my remedies. I must make bandages, I thought, as soon as I finish here.

I did not realise the time passing that stuffy misty day as I worked in my larder. It was past four in the afternoon as I put my medicine jars in order. I was hoping that I would never need the leeches to clean war wounds, when Ruth came through the door, she obviously wanted me to deal with something urgently. It was pleasingly cool in the little stone outhouse and I was reluctant to leave.

"Lady Boyons is here." Ruth pulled open the heavy wooden door. "She needs to speak to you."

I swept angrily past Ruth. "Where is she?" If that woman is going to lecture me on my daughter I wanted to be ready for it.

"In the front parlour madam." She hurried along at my heels.

The Battle of Naseby, 14th June 1645

My husband Lord Howard was sitting astride his handsome roan horse on Dust Hill looking across the field of battle. He was always one for tactics and watching the battle, only joining in the fray if he felt he really needed to. He took an apple from his saddle bag, bit it, pulled a face as he threw it to the ground. "Sour." he spat. "Like our chances here." He turned his horse and signalled his retinue to follow him. The Royalists were outnumbered, he guessed, by at least ten to one. It was time to retreat. The shouts of "Retreat in Good Order" to those who were not already slaughtered were heard echoing across the Royalist lines on the field.

As he turned his horse he saw a tanned, raddled man in a Lobster pot helmet riding a huge chestnut stallion towards him, the sweat and dirt of battle running in rivulets down his face. Behind him marched a regiment of tired war torn men in red coats. They were covered in dirt and blood.

Lord Howard's retreat to Clipston had been halted in it's tracks. "God's breath," Howard swore at his lieutenant. "Cromwell himself."

Howard was staring at the Lieutenant General who was engulfed in raucous laughter. Cromwell pulled his horse alongside Howard's and in almost ridiculous hysteria laughed in his face.

"What are you about?" Howard asked puzzled.

"Winning the war, I can see you are about being a most excellent coward." Cromwell reined his excited horse in. "Take them all prisoner, except for him." He commanded. "I will escort him myself." He leant across and slipped a lead through the bridle of Howard's roan who backed away and started to kick.

"He has more spirit for a fight than you Sir." He pulled the horse to order, took a leather blackjack from his saddlebag and drank deeply from it watching his prisoner from the corner of his eye. "You have not introduced yourself."

"I am Lord Howard, I suppose you are Cromwell, due to your demeanour and manner of dress."

Cromwell laughed again. "Ah, I hear you have a pretty daughter do you not?"

Howard raised his eyebrows in surprise, wondering how he knew.

The Lieutenant General of the Parliament Army had always had an eye for a pretty girl. He had been given a miniature taken from a teenage Lord during the battle. The young woman had been painted pretty, fair and smiling, he had been told it was Lord Howard's daughter. He looked forward to meeting her and her mother when they came to pay the ransom for Howard. Cromwell turned the miniature over in his pocket smiling to himself.

As his captor turned both horses to move on, Howard could see over his shoulder his cavalry had been made to dismount, and common foot soldiers rode their horses while his men were to walk.

His Ensign refused to give up his colours - the tussle soon turned to a fight with Howard's man being beaten by club muskets. Howard turned away trying to close his ears to the screams of his former blacksmith John Bold. There was a crunching of bone as his skull shattered under the continued battery of musket stocks against his head.

"What manner of man are you – if you be a man?" Shouted one of Howard's officers. "Howard!" He screamed. "You bastard."

The winner of Howard's colours boldly tied their flag around his waist. "So I can wipe my arse on the Royalists," he snorted, laughing.

Howard led on, too ashamed to look back at his men, wondering how Cromwell knew he had a daughter, and whether she was pretty or not. It did not occur to him that Cromwell knew where he had been hiding. He suddenly realised he must have done, because he was behind a copse at the top of Dust Hill, hidden from view, waiting with the rest his cavalry to ambush when called on.

On the field nearby a circle of blue coated Rupert's Regiment of Foote were standing hard, back to back, shoulder to shoulder, muskets and swords at the ready. Their ensign in their midst waving their distinctive black and white flag. They shouted "for God and the Cause, the Church and the Laws, Charles, King of England and Prince Rupert of the Rhine!" it was not long before they were surrounded by men and horse circling around them.

"Let us see this play out Lord Coward, they are of your regiment are they not?" Cromwell turned his horse to watch the show. A few Blewcoats managed to retreat by running through the horse's legs. The rest of the Blewcoats, to a man, despite putting up a good fight, were slaughtered where they stood. "Entertaining is it not?" Cromwell laughed spitefully as he pulled both horses to a gallop, leaving Howard in little doubt what his fate would be if he could not be ransomed.

"I am a widow." Lady Boyons' words fell as hard as stone pebbles on my ears. "We were raided last night. They left us just the one old mare, I could not come sooner."

"Katherine?" I asked, my heart frantically pounding in my chest.

"She got away, there is no sign of her at the house." Lady Boyons said.

"Thanks be to God." I offered her a seat beside the fire place. "Tell me all." But I was not steady, I knew what could happen to pretty young girls unprotected.

"My poor husband, cut to pieces seeing to his horses," she sighed. "We heard the horses stamp and cry out, my Lord went to see what was about, a fox or mayhap a boar looking for food among the hay." She took out her kerchief and wiped her eyes, then took a sip of red wine from the glass Ruth had brought for her. "What am I to do?"

"Stay here tonight." I touched her arm gently, although I had no great care for Lady Boyons, I could see by her red eyes that her distress was considerable. "Where are your servants?"

"The old cook dead, her head bashed in for not having any good provender." The lady was now shaking. "Her husband came with me – he is in your kitchen, with your man."

"You cannot leave your house open to all, with bodies strewn about, woman." I stared at her. "Come, tomorrow we will get whatever men we can from the village and go and sort your household."

Carpenter came to the door. "News Madam, a messenger." He said politely as he was on his best behaviour. "The King is in retreat."

I stood up, the day had now gone, the heat cooling down. My mind was reeling. Where was my daughter? My husband? My lover? I clutched the back of the settle and tried to compose myself.

"Which way?" I managed ask.

"Ask him yrself." Carpenter stood aside as Jonathan strode into the room. We gagged at the smell of horse and man sweat, he looked exhausted. Older, by a days frenzied battle.

"Madam, forgive me." He swept a low bow.

"Carpenter, fetch Ruth and Godfrey, we all need to hear this." I remained standing, although I don't know how, underneath my day gown and shift my knees trembled and shook. When the servants were in the room I took it upon myself to fill glasses of wine for everyone much to Lady Boyons' disgust. Becoming a servant myself, to give me a task to distract me.

Jonathan took a draft of his glass. "The King is headed for Leicester this night, with Fairfax in pursuit." He sat on the settle, exhausted. His hollow darkened eyes stared into the empty fire grate. "We have lost." he said bitterly.

"The battle, but not the war – surely?" I asked confused.

He sipped his wine but made no answer.

"How came you here?" Lady Boyons sneered. Although only in her forties Lady Mary Boyons had an unattractive portly little face with a spiteful downward smile. "Cowardly cur."

"With news Madam." Jonathan said, ignoring her slight. "There will be others to come after me, I have a good mare, she's exhausted now, but I felt Lady Howard should be the first to know."

"Know what?" I froze, horrified, dreading the worst.

"Your husband is to be ransomed. Your daughter madam is feared dead."

I drew in my breath and staggered to a chair. "Katherine, my beautiful Katherine." The pain was so great in my chest I thought I was going to die.

I saw a feint smile cross Lady Boyons' lips. I knew at once what she was thinking, her feeble witted son had a second chance for money and heirs.

"My son?" she asked.

"Most of the men on the field who lived were taken prisoner. I imagine he would have been amongst them." Jonathan answered brusquely.

"YOU!" I turned on Lady Boyons, "You told me she was safe."

"Anything she did she brought on herself. I asked her to hide with us, but no, she had to find her own way out. Headstrong as ever. Serves her right." She sipped her wine. "So now I am free of my horrible old husband pawing at me, and my son is free of your barren daughter."

I slapped her face so hard the glass spun across the room and shattered on the stone floor. "Get out of my house." I screamed at her. "Get out!"

"With pleasure, you have just proved every point I have ever made about you and your family." She hissed, "We are pleased to be free of you Madam Farthing for you are nothing to me now!" As she stood up she grabbed old Godfrey's arm and I was pleased to see I had left a livid red hand mark clear on her cheek.

"I am Lady Howard," I retorted angrily, "The King himself gave me my husband."

"A lot of good that did you." She laughed spitefully as she walked towards the door with her old servant.

I fell on the settle with a thump next to Jonathan, his eyes were closing from exhaustion. "I must sleep madam. We will contrive to amend in the morning." He stood up, "Where may I go?"

Ruth dropped a curtsy. "The byre has clean dry straw and a water bucket, I can fetch soap, towel and blanket."

"Thank you Ruth, get our guest some beer, bread and fowl, he must be starving." I managed to choke out. I could see Ruth was tired, it was late and she had been working all day, probably doing Carpenter's work as well as her own.

His exhausted eyes could hardly stay open. "Murder does not give me an appetite madam, but I need to eat to live. So I will thank you, and say God's blessings and goodnight."

He staggered out to the barns, still warm from the summer sun and smelling of sweet hay. He fell into the deep straw and was asleep in a moment.

Almost in a stupor, Ruth placed a basket of bread, chicken, apples, and beer by his side and threw a linen towel over it. She covered his unconscious body with a rough wool blanket from one of the horses. Seeing how sore tired his poor horse was, she put a bucket of water down for it and gave it a handful of oats. After patting it's sweating neck she walked exhausted back into the kitchen. Duties done, she sat at the scrubbed pine table, lay her head on her arms and fell asleep.

Two things I had learnt throughout my life, taking their conjugal rites and killing made men soporific. Both give a certain level of exhaustion and exhilaration that combined to throw them into the arms of Morpheus. I remembered how Howard was when he came back from a hunt. As soon as the venison had be taken to the larder, my Lord would come into the grand dining room happy, hungry and after dinner, falling asleep in his chair in the warmth of the fire.

I put my arms around my knees as I rocked back and forth. My Katherine was not dead, she could not be dead, I would feel it in my heart, here. I put my hand on my chest and felt the steady rhythm of the beat of my heart. I listened in the silence of the house and the late evening birdsong from the gardens outside. She was not dead, I knew it. I was determined. I will find her.

In the barn Jonathan's sleep was fitful. His nightmares tormented him with the voices of the screaming women of the baggage train as they endured a frenzied attack from the Roundheads. Those who could, running away holding their faces, some had their noses cut off, some were cut across their faces, their blood flooding down into the green earth. He could hear the sound of flesh being run through with sword and the crunching of bone as halberds and club muskets feverishly did their work. As men fought to stay alive, the shouts and screams of men women and horses, lying in their death throes, rang in his ears. He relived the cavalry horses over running him. He had screamed in pain as their hooves hit him hard in the back. He lay face down in the mud in a stupor, left for dead.

Men cried to God, prayed. The so called righteous men of God, the Puritans, slit the throats of dying men as they robbed them. Then they raped the bodies of the women of the baggage train, while their terrified, crying, children watched and waited for their own slaughter.

"Dear God! No! No!" Jonathan screamed as he sat up in a sweat.

Ruth was passing with the full milk pail, she sat it in the shade, and popped her head into the barn. Jonathan's heart was pounding fit to burst.

"Sir?" She enquired gently, "need you anything?"

He tried to raise himself on his elbows. "Is it cock crow?" He asked.

"Yes." She opened the door of the barn and a fresh breeze blew through. The green fields of grass rippled in the wind, the hens were clucking in the yard.

He could see the pail full of creamy fresh milk, and Ruth's scrubbed pink face and clean apron. She picked up the pail, her hands were covered with the red cow pox rash from the milking. Behind her the watery blue sky was brightening as the sun rose. The world seemed normal again. He tried not to think of the battlefield strewn with the mutilated bodies of men and women.

"I need to wash, I need salve and bandages." He said as normally as he could. His doublet and the buffcoat that had probably saved his life stunk of horse dung. Blood had been pouring through his linen shirt. The smell of black powder and saltpetre, the devils sulphur was still in his nostrils.

His mind was working feverishly – what now? What now?

The Aftermath

I was bathing Jonathan's wounds with the help of Ruth. The cuts from the horse's hooves ran quite deep, he had sword slashes on his shoulders, arms and chest. We gave him laudanum to help still the pain. After we bound him, we helped him dress in one of my husband's shirts and a pair of breeches. Carpenter had come round after he'd seen the extent of Jonathan's hurts and carried him like a sack of potatoes to the guest room in the manor. He dropped him on the bed and went outside for a smoke of his pipe. Something both Ruth and I recognised as a comfort after being distressed.

Jonathan tossed and turned, "I must go back, I must go back." He muttered.

"When you are recovered." I held his hand, "When you are well."

I didn't ask about Katherine, if I didn't know what happened to her, she could still be alive.

Carpenter came into the room with some gruel. "Aye lass, I made it." He stared at Ruth who had taken over the cook's job. Carpenter's hooded Irish eyes stared at me trying to spoon the soup into Jonathan.

"I'll not tell his Lordship, if I am here when he returns. Count on me." Carpenter watched my face. "I will have to leave, I will be killed if I stay, and you will be killed for harbouring a Catholic."

"But you do not practice." I watched his face. "Where will you go?"

"Home." Carpenter looked at me. "I need fare for the boat and food."

"Of course." I went to my closet and took out three coins, one gold and two silver. "The gold is to set you up at home, so don't drink it, and the silver is to get you there. Take bread, cheese, meat." I stood up to shake his hand. "Be careful Carpenter."

He looked at the money in his hand and quickly stuffed it into his pouch. He turned to Ruth.

"You're a good un." He smiled as he leant and kissed her cheek gently. "Like a daughter to me. I have a daughter your age, and if God spares me I'll see her again."

Ruth touched her cheek surprised.

We heard Carpenter go downstairs and out of the back door. We were now two women alone, undefended and caring for an injured Royalist soldier.

Lady Boyons was jolted slowly towards her ransacked Manor on old Barley. Her husband wasn't a bad man, in fact he was too good. He was sixty years now, suffering from arthritis, but had been still able to ride and work. He was kindly, but an old man. After Richard's birth he had developed a stone in the kidneys. It had stopped their loving, and he could not piss without a servant pouring water and whistling outside the closet door. It had seemed that however she had stroked it, his poor dogge had died.

He battled on, but all pride in himself had gone, he wore tattered work clothes to work on the land with his men. Hardly bathed, just once a year now instead of three. He had decided to become old. Before the war, the servants had called him Kindly Old Dick as he would give them coins from his coffers if they pleaded some need. He also gave them days off to see their parents. All of this riled Mary Boyons, for it was her money he was giving away.

When the King raised his standard at Nottingham Castle and the war started in earnest. Kindly Old Dick had encouraged most of the servants to go and fight for the King, giving each a gold coin for their trouble.

"For God's sake Richard, you will have us as paupers." She had shouted bitterly at him.

He had taken her hands in his and kissed them. "My love, I have a care for us, the money we have left is more than enough, and we many need their favours in the future. Who knows what this war might bring?"

She had sighed heavily. She had promised to love, honour and obey.

"I cannot fight for my old friend Charles my love, but I will send Richard in my stead." He held her to him.

"No," she pushed him away, "No, he's but eighteen and newly wed." She turned her back on him. "Not my Richard."

"He must go dearest heart." The strength in his voice was as such that she knew there would be no arguing. "He's all we have to represent the family, would you have all his friends laugh at him?"

"That barren little bitch he's married – they'll be no more Boyons." She spat harshly.

"Now my love," the old Lord had sat in his favourite chair. "They have been married but a twelvemonth. Time will bring us grandchildren. She is strong and healthy."

Hate and bile towards Katherine rose in Lady Boyons' throat. "Her mother only had one child." She retorted spitefully.

His Lordship had raised his eyebrows in surprise. "So have we sweet love, it means nothing. We both have one living child."

"Whom you are sending away to die." She stamped her foot angrily, "Your only son." Mary's eyes pleaded with her husband. "Please Richard, please, send him away to Holland on some errand."

"No." Lord Boyons stood up. "Woman," he spat angrily, "He must fight under the Boyons flag, for me, for himself and for the King."

So that was the end of it.

As the old horse trudged along, Lady Boyons mind relived the escape from her house through servants corridors hidden behind the tapestries. The sleeping Roundhead Officer was her only obstruction until she reached the passageway to the stairs. She and Godfrey disappeared behind a tapestry of Judith and the Elders and made their way down the cold dusty stairs to the back kitchen where Godfrey's old wife lay dead, her head staved in on the kitchen table. Her cooking not to the Roundhead's liking.

Godfrey gently stroked her white hair as they passed. "God bless um." he whispered.

"Come." His mistress snapped quietly. "Get old Barley out."

Old Barley was an elderly mare that Lord Boyons had loved all his life. Kept now as an expensive pet, the old horse was only too pleased to see anyone. She put up no resistance to having a saddle put on her bowed and aching back.

As they crept away over the brow of the hill towards the Howards' manor house, Lady Boyons felt extremely grateful to her husband's Tudor ancestor who had built the secret passageways in the house. He was close to King Henry, but the King was volatile in his nature. When the house was built it seemed necessary to put escape routes and hidden tunnels, just in case the King's anger was ever vented against his minister.

Over the peaceful years under his daughter Queen Elizabeth the children of the house used them for playing hide and seek.

A widow now, she smiled her thin smile. Twenty years of the old Lord asserting his rights over her were now gone. He was forty when they married, she was his second wife. He was tall and handsome with long brown hair under his burgundy felt hat with white ostrich feathers. She fell for him immediately, an impressionable girl rising seventeen years. The dowry was arranged and they set off on the journey of married life together. Portraits painted by Van Dyke, their first son born dead to their devastation, a daughter taken by the pox at six, followed by the birth of her pride and joy, her son Richard, who she spoiled shamelessly.

So lost in her memories, Lady Mary Boyons had not realised her poor old tired horse had reached the village that surrounded her Manor. Dark smoke rose from many of the houses, winding upwards into the sky. She looked around unable to take in the devastation. Bodies lay everywhere. Old women cradled their defiled and raped daughters and sobbed. Their screams echoing through the street. At the church door, young men were piled in heaps after being executed by musket ball to stop them joining the King. Some were children as young as twelve.

"Dear God in Heaven." Lady Boyons choked, "Look what they have done to our people."

A few battered and wounded old Clubmen had done their best. As they saw her Ladyship pass by, they spat at her and called her names. She had let them down, she had not called on the usual protectors of their village.

She could have paid the mercenaries, sent her man to fetch them. They were only in Woodstock, drinking in the Inns. It was not that far away. Kindly Old Dick would have done it. He knew the village men couldn't better the might of a Puritan army without help. There was just too many of them. They rested on the gravestones in the churchyard watching Lady Boyons pass on her old brown mare.

"Ye could have called on Howards' men, on any countrymen. The mercenaries from Woodstock ye old bitch." One shouted. "Yet ye ran away leaving Kindly Old Dick to die."

She sat on old Barley staring straight ahead, ignoring them as best she could.

The stench of burning wood, blood and sulphur hung in the air. The poor old horse stumbled. Somehow realising it was getting near to home, it tried it's best to get through the bodies and wreckage on the road.

Lady Boyons slid off the mares back to help lighten her load. Tears were running down her face. Her stiff reserve dissolving as they moved forward. Occasionally her shoe would get sucked off in the mire as she made her way through the morass of war.

"We must see to our own," she muttered to herself. She decided she did not hear them shouting at her. However, she had noticed the musket balls that had passed through the heads of the young men that now peppered the old wooden church door with holes. Some of the balls lay still embedded inside the old oak of the door.

"We should turn back." Godfrey stopped the old horse. "Back to the Howards, and safety, I'm afeared of what we will find to home your Ladyship."

"We will not go back to that whore's house." She snapped with a downward smile. "We are free of them, we will not go back."

As they left the village, they found the road leading towards the manor had been churned to deep mud courtesy of the feet of hundreds of marching Parliamentarian soldiers, their cavalry, cannon and the baggage train. Lady Boyons was not one to be gainsaid by events, so they trudged on.

Jonathan was sitting up in bed with a thumping headache. Every part of his body ached. I went up to see him to take him a small beer and some bread and cheese.

"How are you today?" I asked sitting closely beside him so that I could smell if any of his wounds had gangrene. I put the tray on his lap.

"Everything hurts." He looked up at me. "But I must go back."

"Tis over," I passed him the beer. "I heard a rumour the King is headed for Hampton Court and London. "Twas a terrible defeat."

"How long have I been here?" He asked, worried.

"Only two days." I replied, "When you are rested, we must try and find my daughter."

"She must be dead, I could find no trace of her anywhere." Jonathan rubbed his jaw, it still had a massive bruise from a musket stock.

"No," I broke the bread for him and buttered it, "I would know."

"Lord Howard?" He asked watching my face.

"Ransomed." I stood up, "I had the note yesterday, from Cromwell himself."

I rifled in my pouch and gave it to him to read.

"Can you afford this?" He asked.

"I cannot pay it." I walked to the door, "I will not pay it. Eat and rest, for by the end of the week we are leaving to find Katherine."

"No sooner, we must not let them outride us." Jonathan sat up, his face grey with pain, "We must go as soon as I can stand."

I asked Ruth if she had any family who could help look after my house. She ran down to our village and came back with her mother and father and two younger brothers.

"Them Roundhead's 'ave burnt my barns and taken the stock." Ruth's father was a gnarly farmer of about forty. "The boys and mother were hid watching them. They were renegades, coming to us by way of being lost." He sighed, "Thank God they knew not the hidden copse."

Ruth pulled a stout, broad faced, friendly looking woman in a dirty apron forward. "Lady Howard, this is my mother Alice, and these are my brothers," Two tall gangly youths of about fourteen and sixteen gave a bow to me. "George and Frank."

"Missus." They mumbled, both were covered in mud from hiding in the undergrowth.

"You have a home here now." I watched their faces. "Be good to me and I will be good to you."

"Than'en yow." Ruth's father bowed to me, "I be George the elder."

"Come to the kitchen." I ordered. They sat around the table looking at all the pewter plates and cooking pots, they seemed in awe of their new surroundings, appreciating everything.

"I have to go and try to find a ransom for Lord Howard. I also have to find my daughter Katherine." I walked to Ruth and put my hand on her shoulder. "Ruth has worked here for nearly two years, she knows how things are to be done. She has worked here, when we had a house full of servants, to today when we have none." I walked round the family. "Come what may I will look after you if you look after me."

The kitchen door burst open with a bang making us all jump.

"Room for one more?" Carpenter stood tall and battered with fewer teeth than he had when he left a week ago. "I knows the ropes so to speak."

"What happened to you?" Ruth asked watching his cut face.

"Aye, I wanted to see me daughter, but the Roundhead's wanted to hang me for being a Catholic, then the Royalists rescued me and recruited me to be a pikeman. So I made me own choice, to come back here till the war is over."

"I'm glad you did." I beckoned him in and he sat at the head of the table while I closed the door behind him.

"What news?" I asked, "Where are the armies now?"

"Cromwell is headed west and the King is headed south." He leant forward as if telling a great secret, "wherever you go there are stragglers, skirmishes, wounded on the road. This damned country is not safe for man nor beast. Over seven hundred souls are left to rot on the field." When Carpenter was satisfied he had scared us all enough, he sat back in his chair sucking what was left of his teeth.

"Ruth get your family washed, properly dressed and fed." I looked at her sternly." She smiled at me, "May I use the old servants fustian clothes in the attic?"

I nodded and the family disappeared chattering excitedly amongst themselves. Carpenter nodded to me and walked to the yard to pick up his snapsack and bag.

"We will need disguises." I stared at Jonathan. "What think you?"

"You will need to hide your precious items, money and jewels, before we get to disguises." He got up stiffly, I helped him by putting my arm under his shoulders.

"In the crypt of our church on the estate." I volunteered.

"That will be the first place they look." A weak smile crossed his face, "Everyone does that my love in the hope the dead will not be desecrated. Tis well known."

"My love?" I queried, watching his face.

"Tes not the time. I have a plan. We need flour sacks and rope. We also, unfortunately, need someone to climb on the roof, which I cannot do."

Naseby Field after the Battle

Katherine slid off her horse and slapped him hard across his haunches. "Home Balthazar." She whispered huskily in his ear before he cantered off. She watched, crippled with pain, as he raced off in the direction of Lady Boyons' Manor. She dragged her bruised and bleeding body through the heaving mass of humanity and dying horses. There were so many that they were lying almost head to tail on the grass.

The field was strewn with crying women and dead soldiers. Some Parliament looters were picking the pockets and stripping the bodies of anyone who looked to own anything they could sell. So Katherine reasoned she was walking through the Royalist dead.

A few soldiers were walking through the bodies inspecting the wounded. Those who were able to survive by their reckoning found themselves thrown on a cart to be taken to where the Royalist survivors would be treated in a makeshift hospital near Northampton. Those too badly injured were put to the sword to save their suffering. She shuddered as she heard a man scream.

"No! No!" As his life ended in a gush of blood from his throat. She clutched her stomach, it was bad enough having her courses and the cramps that accompanied them, without the pain of the stab wounds she had suffered at the hands of the sergeant in the stables.

She walked through the women of the Royalist Baggage train, many of whom had been raped and murdered. Those who were still alive were huddled under the wheels of their overturned wagons. Some had their faces slashed and some had lost their noses. Children screamed and clutched at her, asking for help, she pulled away from them.

She turned over a few bodies, those who had similar hair, build and coat colour to her husband. She was exhausted, there must have been at least four thousand bodies on this field. As twilight fell, all hope deserted her. She decided to go to the Roundhead's camp and give herself up. Perhaps they would kill her quickly.

She was dressed in the sergeant's stinking uniform, which was an offence in itself. As she headed up the hill towards the gate guards tent at the campsite, she could see the light from a brazier and the white of the tent against the darkening sky. She struggled towards the enemy. I don't care about anything any more, she thought, as she rubbed her hand over her face. Unknowingly she had soon covered her pretty face with mud and blood.

"Who goes there?" The gate guard shouted as she staggered towards him. He saw a lanky lad, obviously badly wounded, wearing the new model army breeches and a blood stained shirt.

She tried to reply but a horrible guttural sound came out "Ephrahim." It was the only puritan name she knew, it had belonged to one of her mother in law's stable lads.

She lunged into the light of the lanterns hanging on the posts. She had stuffed her long curled hair into a montero, a woollen cap with a peak that she had taken from her dead attacker's balding head.

"Where's your coat?" He walked towards the gawky lad, who seemed to be bleeding from everywhere.

"Lost it fighting," she choked out, which was true. She dropped down on to a log near the fire and sat on it. She was feeling cold, she was losing so much blood she was feeling faint. Falling in and out of consciousness, she closed her eyes as she relived the attack from the sergeant. His filthy grasping hands all over her body, one hand holding the knife to her neck, while the other explored his prize. She screamed and tried to turn, her husband's faithful horse Balthazar had reared during the attack, pounding the man's back and tearing his red coat off him.

"Beer." The gate guard offered her his blackjack.

"No." She choked as she showed him the strangle marks and cuts of the blade around her neck.

"Ah, ye must try lad. Try." She was desperately thirsty and tried to drink the beer, but it came up immediately covered in blood. She spat it into the fire making the flames flare in the semi-darkness. She wiped her mouth with the back of her hand.

She closed her eyes again with the pain. Suddenly the sergeant's rough rugged features were in front of her again. She had twisted round to face him frantically trying to get the dagger from his hand. Balthazar pushed forward violently, the sergeant's chest gave a sickening thud against the dagger in her hand as he was pushed against it. She pushed it up into his ribs. She had never killed anything before, but as his own dagger slid into his ribs, she found she was surprised how easy it was to kill a man.

She had taken clothes from his bedroll, they were slightly cleaner than the ones he was wearing, but they still stank of stale sweat. As she dressed, for the first time in her life, she was pleased she was flat chested. Her tight bodices had always given her little paps a lift and a curve, but without them she was flat as a pancake.

She came to again to hear the gate guard calling down the camp. "Call for the Doctor, Doctor to the Gate." The message was passed on by rowdy voices, in between the loud singing of hymns, thanking God for their victory.

The Puritan Army was strangely proficient with caring for the injured. Some two hundred wounded Royalist prisoners had been taken by cart to Northampton to be treated. Their own treated at the camp for the moment.

Katherine sat, her head spinning, watching the flames in the brazier. A man wearing a grey curled wig and blued back and breast, ran over to her. "What's to do?"

"Him be strangled sur, and spittin' up blud." The gate guard said helpfully.

Dr John Bastwick pulled the young lad's face upwards, his neck was livid red with cuts and strangle marks. The first thing he noticed was that there was no Adam's apple. He put his arm under the boy's shoulder. "He's ruptured his Adam's apple," he concluded. "I'll take him with me."

"Lord keep ye, lad, you'm in safe hands now." The gate guard swigged his beer from the jug, leaving the blooded blackjack on the grass where the lad had dropped it.

Katherine limped alongside the Doctor, past the hospital tent where men were crying and screaming in pain. "Oh God preserve us." One rough voice called out. They were almost drowned out by the hymns of praise coming from the rest of the camp to the God who had chosen the Parliament Army over the Royalists.

"Where are we going?" She choked out, scared for the life that she'd wanted to end just an hour ago.

"You'll see," The old Doctor answered kindly.

"I need to go home." She tried to pull away but was too weak.

"Take heed woman, you will die if the throat is not treated, if that doesn't kill you tis certain one of these men will." He held her tightly.

"What?" she asked terrified.

"Listen," he whispered as they got nearer to his tent in a quieter part of the camp. "I am a Doctor trained in Padua, I know a woman when I see one." He dragged her towards a large tent, "You do not need to tell me what you've been through, for I can guess. But do tell me, were you with the Royalist Baggage – are you Catholic?"

"No, I was taken from home when the Army passed through yesterday." She coughed, blood splattered her stolen shirt. "I am a good protestant woman." The coughing got worse.

"Hush, hush." He sat her in a folding chair, closed the tent flap and laced it shut. "These men are like all men at war, God has nothing to do with the evil they do in his name. I could not in all faith leave you to them."

He took off his armour and hung it on a wooden stake pushed into the ground. He took off his wig and put a black-work embroidered cap on his head. His own hair covered his face, he had a black moustache and goatee, but she noticed, he was missing his ears. She couldn't ask, but knew this was a sign of a dissident.

"I am the Captain of the Leicester Trained Bands now, but have other plans," he waffled on. He rifled through his well provisioned medicine box, took a small bottle, mixed some ingredients, and shook the bottle well. He guided her into a wooden folding campaign arm chair. She sat obediently, too sick to do much else. Her frightened eyes watched as he removed her stinking boots and hose, to show her feet cut to pieces by the rough seams of the hard leather of the bucket boots as they rubbed against her toes. He took a cooling lavender salve and, after washing her feet, applied this to the cuts. "Jesus of Nazareth washed the feet of his disciples, so I do for you." She nodded, tired, unable to speak, but her eyes said volumes.

"What happened to the man who owned these clothes?" He asked as he treated her.

"Dead. Horse killed him." She rasped, blood pouring from her mouth again.

"Speak no more, drink this." He gave her the tincture he had made. "It will burn, but your throat will mend."

She gulped it down. Surprisingly it stayed down.

The Doctor took a shirt with a plain collar from his shirt press. "Twas my sons, put it on after I have dressed your wounds." He pulled the blood soaked shirt from her body. She was covered in cuts and bruises, he washed her with salt water, then rubbed her back with some alcohol from his bottle by the bed. "Will stop the wounds turning bad." He explained as he worked on her. While he worked professionally on her snow white skin, she felt no embarrassment. She no longer cared that this man was seeing her naked from the waist up. When she had the shirt on, he pulled the Montero from her head, her beautiful golden curls cascaded over the shoulders of the white shirt. "This I must do if you wish to live." He took some scissors from his bag. She nodded, and he started to cut her hair, giving her the Roundhead's distinctive style. He threw her curls onto the brazier in the tent and they sizzled as they burnt.

"Mistress." He whispered, "Trust me to help you, your breeches must come off. I have no motive but to heal a young woman who has been brutally abused by our men." He stood up and took some plaister jars and bandages from his medicine cabinet. "It is a small recompense for me, so that when my time comes, I might yet get to see the face of our Lord."

Katherine stood up and hung her head in shame as she untied the cord around the waist holding the breeches up. The shirt covered her modesty a little. They fell to the floor, her long white legs were covered in blood.

"God's life, how are you alive?" His cold hands bathed the cuts at the top of her thighs and applied plaisters, smoothing the cold liquid over the cuts and waiting till it set.

"Courses." She mumbled embarrassed. The doctor made a rough pad for her and after washing her, put it between her legs. Tears ran down her flushed face. She started to shake.

The Doctor stood up and turned his back so that she could arrange her intimate garments, "He was going to rape you, saw your courses making you unclean so cut your thighs for if he was caught, he could say it was your wounds." The Doctor's shoulders heaved in despair.

She nodded. "Tis so. Such a Godly man." She coughed, the blood from her mouth was a little less now. Katherine closed her eyes, remembering the frenzied attack by her horse

Balthazar. He had saved her from the worst of the sergeant's intentions. She herself made sure he would never do anything of the like again. She shivered.

The Doctor threw her a pair of clean breeches from his clothes chest. She put them on. "Take my son's couch he'll not be back this night." He led her to a camp bed. "Rest if you can, I must do my rounds."

He washed his hands under a jug of water after throwing the rest of her clothes onto the fire making it smoke. She pulled the thin blanket over her shoulders and turned her back to the brazier. The Doctor made up another bottle of his medicine and put it on the table beside her. He tapped it with his finger. "For morning. I'll take these boots to give to the gate guard as a reward. Rest, for you will be saved." Dr John Bastwick laced up his tent and bustled out to do his rounds.

Katherine was so exhausted she fell asleep, her pains easing. She felt safe in the old Doctor's care. Even the rowdy carousing of her enemies could not keep her awake.

It was because Dr John Bastwick was one of the best physician surgeons in England, that he ended up as a Captain in the Parliament Army. A Leveller sympathiser and a Rebel, his ears had been cut off for sedition, he and his family had been imprisoned until the start of the war, it was not so very bad he thought, it gave him a chance to write.

As the war broke out he was released to Captain Leicester's regiment. Cromwell needed a physician to hand who was a least as good as the Royal Doctor, Sir William Harvey.

However, his re-instatement made him more brazen and Cavalier in his attitude to the Parliament cause. He had already decided to help this young woman find who she was looking for. The previous day he had disguised his son as a journeyman and sent him home to his mother. Why should he die needlessly in this stinking quagmire of Godless humanity?

If the men did not interest him, their injuries did. He found he was learning new treatments every day. When the war was over he would take his notes to the Royal College of Physicians. He had already planned not to stay long, this bloodbath was not for a man of his religious sensibilities.

He walked amongst the men moaning and crying out for help, some of them were not as badly wounded as the young woman lying quietly on his son's camp bed in his tent. He did what he could, told the apothecaries what to administer to the men and to whom, then made his way back through the camp.

The Road to Leicester, 17th June 1645

It was stiflingly hot as we made our way along the dusty roads to Leicester. Local gossip had told us that both the King and Cromwell were now headed in the same direction. I sat in front on our great horse. Jonathan, who was disguised as my servant, sat behind me. Under a pretence I had managed to get passes to visit my sister in law. I had told the powers that be, that she was incommoded by the late birth of a child. I, being a well known midwife, was allowed to go and help her to deliver my brother's heir.

My straw hat did nothing to stop the heat. It was constantly annoying, bumping poor Jonathan's head as he sat behind me. Our hope was to find Cromwell to beg for the freedom of my husband, and hopefully find Katherine along the way.

The hedges were full of blossom, swallows flew over the fields catching their dinner mid air. We had ridden for some three hours and we were both getting short tempered and thirsty in the heat. The horse moved forward to drink from a pond near the side of the road. As we had stopped, I took the chance to ask a farmer in a cotton smock, leaning on a fence nearby, where we were. He ignored me. His nut brown face, raddled by the sun, looked up at Jonathan.

"Where is you'm going?" He asked, he had no teeth and his gums looked red raw.

I nudged Jonathan. "Leicester, this lady's sister in law is in need of a midwife."

"You'm a midwife?" He looked up at me, I nodded in agreement knocking my straw hat back off my head. "Your missus be too high born for that." He looked at Jonathan.

"She's not my wife. I work for her," he snarled. "Many a rogue on these roads."

"Aye, aye." The old farmer nodded in agreement.

I slid off the horse, dipped my straw hat into the water, shook it and put it back on my head, as I had seen many women working in the fields do the same on a hot summers day. He stared at me recognising what marked me for one of the lower classes.

"You'm mighty dainty baint ya?" He asked grinning toothlessly at me.

I went to my pack and pulled out a small bottle of clove water. "You have sore gums." I walked closer to the old man, "Tell me where we are and I can give you this medicine for them."

He looked me up and down, weighing up his options. I took some and rubbed it on my gums, the cloves had an immediate numbing effect, so I knew it would work on this suspicious old farmer. "See, will do you no harm."

"You be five miles clear of Market Harborough, straight on this road." He pointed to the dust track ahead of us. "The King be headed that way, saw im not a day since. So depending on your persuasion, head ye to Market Harborough or take the fork in the road before the town to Leicester and Cromwell. Either way be danger."

"Here," I handed him the clove water, "rub on your gums morning and night, will ease the soreness."

He took it, tried it immediately, copying what I had done. "God bless ee mistress, tis the first relief I've had for many a day." He pulled at a non existent forelock in salute of us. I used a mounting stone set at the side of the road by the pond to get back on our horse. Jonathan was soon up behind me, he slapped the reins on the bay's neck and we trotted on towards Market Harborough.

"How long will it take till we get there?" I asked.

"Five miles, about an hour or so." He answered, "Have you any small beer left? I am parched." I passed him my leather bottle.

I heard him drink and sigh with relief, he passed the bottle back, I drank a little and put the cork back in.

I leant back onto his chest. "Am I hurting you?" I asked aware of his wounds.

"No," he slid his arm around my waist, "the only pain will come when we free your husband. Then madam, it will be in my heart."

"Silly boy!" I laughed. "What do you wish?" I turned to look over my shoulder at him, he surprised me by kissing me tenderly on my lips.

"To be with you always, to love you." He sounded sad. "Kind and as loving as you are, you can never be mine."

"I can have no childer. I am older, but perhaps no wiser than you." I took my hat off and carried it by the ties over my arm. I pulled my scarf around my coif, the sun was dropping and it was getting cooler.

"From my experience of being a child, children are not for me, I have no need to leave an heir. Heir to what? Hard work, soldiering, servitude?" He squeezed my waist. "Loving and warmth is my need." He kissed my cheek.

As we talked together on the hot dusty road, it felt no time at all until we reached the outskirts of the town.

"Halt – who goes there?" A soldier in a Bluecoat with a black eye stopped us as we drew near to the town. He put his halberd across the road stopping our progress.

"Tom, is that you? Praise be to God, is the King hereabouts?" Jonathan jumped off the horse's back to slap the young man's shoulders and clasp him to his chest.

"He's here for a night, tomorrow we move to Ashby de la Zouche." We needed food, drink and to keep away from Fairfax. "I am to be on guard to await my turn for food to be brought."

"How long? For you look to have nothing." Jonathan looked at the lad.

"Over two hours." He looked over Jonathan's shoulder, to me on the horse. "Is that your mother?"

"Shh, that's Lady Howard, she's looking for her husband and daughter." He looked at me and smiled, "She took me on when I was injured. How many left?" He asked, his face growing serious.

"Sir John Russell was injured, he is here. Prince Rupert, Prince Maurice, and of course the King."

"Thank 'ee Tom." Jonathan shook the young man's hand. "Need you anything?" he asked.

"Have you any provender? For I have lost all and mayhap they've forgotten me." The young man watched eagerly as Jonathan brought out a small loaf and a chunk of cheese and gave it to him. "We have not much ourselves, will that do?"

The young man suddenly pulled a knife from his pocket and held it to Jonathan's throat. "Coward, you ran, you left us. What more do you have?" I clicked my tongue, the horse moved forward and I kicked the knife from the young man's hands.

"You are here – did you run? The King shall hear of this." I dug my knees into the horse's flank to make him move. Jonathan quickly moved behind Tom pulling his arm up behind his back painfully.

"No mistress, I am desperate. I have not been paid or have eaten for two days." His hollow eyes looked up at me.

"So you would kill a friend?" I asked him watching his face.

"Forgive me, forgive me, I am ravaged, I know not what I do." He squealed in pain.

"Do you trust him Jonathan?" I asked.

"He was a good man once, we all were." He looked his friend in the eyes by pulling his head back. I pulled a coin from my pouch and held it in front of him. "God's truth, you will leave us peaceful?"

"I will I will, please lady." Jonathan let him go and gave him the coin.

"We are not all savages." He whispered to Tom. "This lady saved my life," he pulled his shirt apart at the neck, unhealed wounds with prints of horse's hooves stood out on his shoulders. "I owe her, now you owe her."

"Jonathan, tell no-one of this," Tom was shaking, "friend, please."

Jonathan released his grip on the man's arm, picked up the bread and cheese from the grass and dusted it off. The ferocious look in his eyes as he handed it to Tom made him shiver.

"Go peaceful, the King is quartered at the Cherry Tree Inn." Tom said as he bit the fresh bread, it was good on an empty stomach. He tore it in half to save some for later, he pushed it and the cheese into his snapsack, carefully putting the coin into his empty pouch and pulling the ties tight.

I will be all right, he thought to himself. I am a good man. I was a carpenter like the good Lord, I will be good again. He tried to close out the murders he committed on the field, the contorted faces, the screams. I am a good man. He said again and again, comforting himself with those thoughts as he watched us trot off in the direction of the Cherry Tree Inn.

When we entered, the King was upstairs sitting at a table with his commanders discussing how the young Prince Charles was to be smuggled to the coast and sent to his mother in Holland. I curtseyed to him and Jonathan bowed low, he walked backwards to let me go to the King. He had dark rings under his eyes, his cheeks hollow, but when he saw me he brightened up.

"Lady Howard, my good friend, my dear friend." He smiled at me and I saw a flash of the King I knew from my Oxford days. He stood up and came over to me.

"Your Majesty." I curtseyed again. "I have come to ask for your help."

He walked back behind the table and shrugged his shoulders, "I cannot even help myself madam, for I have lost everything. My baggage was taken, my letters, my gold, it is all gone." He turned towards me, palms down on the table. "So pray, how do you think I can help you?" His sharp features seemed pained.

"I have come to try and find my husband and daughter." I walked over to him, "I wondered if you had seen Lord Howard."

"Certainly not on the field." Prince Rupert laughed spitefully. "He did not die with his men." Rupert was a stunningly handsome man, his dark hair curled long across his shoulders, his eyes bright with mischief. A man's man, I had heard him called. Also a women's man, by all accounts, for the amount of bastards he had begotten.

"Whatever he is, he is my husband." I choked out insulted. "The King brought us together, and no man can put us asunder."

"More's the pity." Rupert smiled as he looked me up and down.

Jonathan's hand gently rested on the hilt of his sword, enough of a signal to Rupert, who smiled a knowing smile I did not like.

"Please fetch the Lady Howard a chair." The King stuttered. One was provided opposite him. "So we presume madam that Old Noll has your husband, so it is to him you must appeal. Get what you can from the meeting and let me know what you hear around his camp."

"I am to be a spy again Sire?" I asked. "Is there any news of my daughter? I know that Lady Boyons Manor was ransacked, her servants killed, her livestock taken. My poor daughter was there." I reached for my kerchief and wiped my eyes, "Sir, this war is very cruel on all of us."

"We caught a Roundhead soldier trying to sell a cream silk dress along the roadside, he was a turncoat, he had been at the Boyons Manor." One of the soldiers standing by the door volunteered. "The murder there was too much even for him. He being a truly Godly man, he ran away and joined us, after a little persuasion." He watched my face as it drained of colour, "I am sorry to say madam that apart from her Ladyship and her old retainer, he said everyone there was killed."

The blood rushed in my ears, my eyes swam with tears. "Katherine, Katherine," I whispered, remembering her dancing about in her lovely cream silk before she set off to see her mother in law.

The King himself patted my hand. "Now madam, keep your hope, in war there is no reason, but there are sometimes miracles."

Prince Rupert opened the door for us, our interview was over, my sobs had quelled it.

"We will see you before you see Cromwell, I think." The Prince whispered to me. "You may bed with me tonight madam if you need comfort."

"Thank you sir, but when I bed a man, I want my mind to be on him, on the pleasure I can give him. Thinking of my daughter would put an end to it." I looked up into his eyes and smiled, touching him gently on his arm. I could see the Prince was surprised and pleased by my comments. So was I, I could still play a man, make him want me.

As we made our way downstairs, Jonathan was sullen. "What in Gods name was that?"

"It is called manipulation, I can tease and not give, but if he thought I might... well, let's see if that brings Prince Rupert to my heels."

Jonathan smiled, "The town is full, we have nowhere to bed. So what think you now?"

"I think we will find a place." I smiled at him. "You will sleep, but I must pay."

A few moments later Prince Rupert's equerry raced down the stairs after us.

"The Prince has offered you his room milady, he will share with his brother Prince Maurice," he gasped, "You sir, are to bed with us in the stables." He stared at Jonathan.

"I should like to sleep at my Lady's door." Jonathan snapped. "For her protection."

The young equerry smiled, "The Prince himself will be protection enough. Come follow me."

I turned on the stairs, a grubby maid beckoned me to one of their best rooms. It was panelled, the bed's four posts were nailed to the ceiling where a dusty russet hanging was the only form of decoration. The bedclothes looked clean, I pulled back the covers, no yellow marks, I brushed the bed with my hand, no crawlers moved through the straw underneath me.

I was exhausted and my mind was racing. Perhaps Katherine had got away, that soldier did not know her by sight. I unlaced my sweat stained stays and threw them on a chair. I unbuttoned my skirt and lay it over the chair with my bodice. I kept my shift on to sleep in. Swords and doublets lay on the floor; Rupert's room, I reminded myself. A candle and pewter tankard sat beside the bed on a small table. I scratched the flint in the tray and lit the candle, it was tallow. Cheap, and smelt of cow fat, but at least it was light.

I got into the bed, but exhausted as I was, I knew I was due no rest. It wasn't long before I felt the sheets lift and a body slide in behind me. I could tell by his fragrance it wasn't Jonathan. Soap, sweat and lavender mixed with an almost overpowering French perfume.

Rupert wound his strong muscular arms around my waist.

I turned to face him. "Ho sir."

He stroked my hair off my face, curled and full like his. "I have come to comfort you Lady Anne."

The darkness in the room was like being smothered with black velvet, only the poor flickering candle showed half light on our faces.

Two Cavaliers forehead to forehead, one in a sweat stained shift, the other in a clean white shirt that smelt of soap.

His young, handsome face moved closer to my older one to kiss it. His brown eyes looked into my blue. I closed my eyes as he kissed me passionately. I knew I could not say no to a Prince.

My memories raced back to the first Prince who had kissed me, now long dead. Another golden boy full of promise, another lifetime ago when I was an innocent young girl hiding from my mother in a Summer garden at Theobalds Palace.

I saw him wince in pain as he moved.

"Your shoulders hurt my Lord," I whispered against his soft lips. "From lifting the sword in full armour for so long today."

He held my wrists tightly and was about to move on top of me when I smiled at him. "You will not fight me then?" he asked.

"There is no need, I am not expecting you to do me a hurt, quite the opposite." He released my wrists and I stroked his face gently. I felt him relax. I gently traced my tongue along his lips before I kissed him. "I have made a cooling salve that will ease your muscles, I will get it afterwards and rub your back."

"Afterwards?" His clipped German voice sounded surprised. "You are most forward madam."

He slipped my shift from my shoulders, and traced my breasts with his fingers then kissed each in turn. I sighed with what I hoped he would perceive as delight.

"What manner of woman are you?" he asked as he painfully bit my shoulder, marking me as his.

"I am a married woman with experience of men. A midwife, there is nothing that I do not know about the act of love." My mouth found his, as we kissed intensely again, a little worm of delight and passion was starting to grow in me.

"Your daughter?" He moved to stroke down my stomach.

"Is alive, despite my tears, I feel she is alive." I put my hand over his mouth which made his dogge grow hard. Now, I know what he likes, I thought to myself, with any good fortune I shall have him spent and I can sleep at last. He was about to move on top of me, but I smiled and sat across his hips. "Let me do the work to save your shoulders, in the new French style."

My head fell back as I rode him, I could feel my soft hair bouncing on my back, he was biting his lip to stop his moment. He was experienced, I knew that. He held my waist tightly, as I pretended fulfilment, he followed immediately after.

"What age are you?" He sighed. "I cannot make you out, your waist is small, your paps are fine."

"Old enough to be your mother, old enough to know better." I climbed off him and put my road stained shift on. I got out of bed and headed for my saddle bag.

"Do you leave me madam?" He had propped himself up on his elbows. "I have given you no permission to go."

"The liniment sire," I ruffled through my bag in the darkness, "for your back and shoulders dear Prince."

I looked at it in the moonlight of the window to check it was the right one, then climbed back into the bed, warm and wet from our loving.

He turned his back to me and I massaged the hard knots of his shoulders until they disappeared under my fingertips.

"I must sleep." I whispered tiredly.

Rupert was already in the arms of Morpheus, face down, gently snoring into the pillow. The same as every man whose business upon a woman is done.

I heard the town clock strike one as I curled up under the covers. The candle had burnt out. An owl hooted mournfully into the dark night. My dreams were full of the dead bodies by the roadside crying out for help. I had heard Cromwell had littered the dusty highways with them. I shuddered. So much death.

Rupert felt the movement and gathered me to him, hugging me as a child hugs his favourite toy. "Fear not my lady," he said drowsily, not waking, "for I am here."

Leicester, June 1645

Oliver Cromwell was hunting, not men this time, but rabbits and pigeons. His falcon flew high into the bright blue sky, it had found it's mark. It hovered, it's wings fluttering as it balanced in the breeze, its bright eyes down ready to stoop. One small movement in the grass below and it would drop like a stone. Talons extended to grip it's victim, it's sharp yellow beak would rip out the throat of it's prey. Oliver could see little, but thought it must be a rabbit or a hare. He was proud of this bird, he had seen it take bigger animals without a problem.

It was only recently that he was able to afford to run two birds, the other, a Merlin, still needed training to the whistle, but was coming along nicely. Oliver Cromwell reflected on his obsession with hawking, it was a lot like this war he was fighting with this petty stuttering King, ruled by his French Catholic wife. Chase. Catch. Kill. He smiled thinking that he would let no woman tell him what to do again.

He thought back to that night in the Library at Ripley Castle where Lady Jane Ingilby held him at pistol point throughout the night. Not even allowing him to relieve himself. If he ever got a chance to corner that fat bitch at Ripley again, he would reward the Catholic harridan with a slit throat. All in the past, he thought, behind me now. He smiled trying to relax and watch his bird at work.

He did not understand women, his own dear wife Elizabeth was a simpleton who could be soothed with a few tender words. She was never a great beauty, and there was never a great passion between them. A worm of jealousy grew in his stomach as he thought of the King and Queen and Fairfax and his wife Anne. There was passion for both of those couples, but what good would it do them? It could only cause pain. Elizabeth brought money and connections, a good family to buy into. She was not bred to run a farm and family, but it was something she did well. She took to it like a duck to water. He smiled, there may not have been passion but when he had needs she obliged him, she had given him fine sons and daughters, so he had no cause for complaint.

Suddenly the falcon dropped from the sky letting out a a loud screech as it fell on it's prey. He could see fur and feathers fly up from the long grass as he ran across to see what he had caught.

The screaming stopped. Silence. A pair of intelligent brown eyes met his. A dog fox held his falcon in his mouth as a large hare bolted for safety through the field. He had the falcon by it's broken neck and it hung like a hanged man in a noose.

Infuriated, Cromwell shouted for his musket. The young man who had accompanied him to carry his bags threw the musket to him. He caught it one handed, had it on his shoulder in a moment, and gave fire.

He missed, the large fox dodged and weaved through the long grass and into the hedges with it's prey before turning and looking at Oliver. He thought it was smiling at him.

"This is a warning from our Lord God!" He expounded, "I have been in the sin of pride." His young attendant looked shocked at Cromwell as he fell to his knees.

"Almighty God, Forgive me for the sin of pride, thank you for punishing me for it." He started to say "Our father," but thunder cracked across the hot summer sky and large drops of rain started to fall. So he got up and started to walk from the fields.

As Oliver made his way back to the town he thought of the other sins he had committed. But as the Almighty God was on his side he felt he had already been forgiven. He was in righteousness.

As they neared the outskirts of the town, Oliver saw Black Tom's horse in a stable by the Inn, an ominous crack of thunder split the darkness with a fork of bright lightening.

It's a warning, he thought to himself. Fairfax may not be true to our cause, the Lord himself is telling me to watch him, keep him close. He wears his hair like a Cavalier, his wife is related to Royalist families, perhaps this is all an adventure to him. Perhaps it is he who wishes to replace the King. The rain started to fall heavily as Cromwell ran into the Inn, he stood for a moment, his paranoia growing with his jealousy of Black Tom as he watched the rain fall.

Royalist Prison,

Leicester Castle, 18th June 1645

In the darkness of the cold prison cell Richard Boyons, unknowingly the new Lord of Boyons Manor in Oxfordshire, lay his lanky frame against the foul smelling wall. He had been taken as a prize and immediately robbed of what little possessions he carried. Even the portrait of his wife Katherine in it's little gold frame had been wrenched from his hand and given to Cromwell.

His company had been attacked on the field, his colours taken.

"To wipe my arse on it." Shouted the Roundhead waving the Boyons family insignia in his face. His regiment, to a man, had been destroyed. He had been saved to be ransomed. That was until Cromwell had found out that Boyons Manor had already been raided and anything of worth, taken. He closed his eyes as he replayed the moment again and again. He had not been a coward, he had fought well, but they had been outnumbered three to one. There was no hope. He had watched with empty eyes as his men were killed around him, fighting to the last, screaming in anger and pain. The horses strangled cries were worse than the mens. At least the men knew what they were fighting for. But the dumb animal's huge glassy eyes stared at him in his dreams as they lay writhing in their own blood.

The few gold coins his father had given him were ripped from his leather purse around his waist.

He lay head back, looking out of the barred window into a blue sky. Swallows reeled overhead, their cries of a Summer to come a small matter comforting.

He was listless, now he was of no worth, he was waiting to be shot.

The cell door was opened with a loud bang, another prisoner was thrown into the stinking darkness. Richard recognised the man immediately, it was his father in law.

"My God sir, Lord Howard, it is you!" He exclaimed with more joy than he felt.

The men clasped each other in greeting.

"What news of Katherine?" Richard asked urgently. "My family?"

Lord Howard sat on the stinking straw. His son in law joined him.

"Of Katherine, I know not, but I hope." He sighed, "It is possible she is dead."

Richard's face dropped. Suddenly he did not look like a young man.

"Your mother still lives, but your Manor is sacked, all your livestock taken, your father and servants killed." Lord Howard took his cream kid gloves off and wiped his sweating forehead with his hand.

"I knew most of it." Richard said sadly,

"The soldiers boast of your father's riches, I have heard them talk of how they took your good horses and muskets. How the Boyons' fat geese will feed Cromwell. All who were there have a crown from your father's chest." He sighed.

Richard smiled sadly remembering his generous father. "Had they but asked he would have given it to them freely to save the household. He was as kind as my mother was mean."

"I have never heard you talk ill of Lady Boyons lad," Lord Howard lay back on the cold damp wall, his eyes closed.

"I'm about to die, it's time to be honest. Mother is one of the devil's own, she's too evil to die, she will survive us both." He said sorrowfully. "The devil would not have that old harridan in his ranks telling him what to do."

"There was an old farmer who had such a wife," sung Lord Howard, "Who harried and pestered him for the whole of his life." Both men were soon singing a ribald song to the tune of Lilliburlero, laughing hysterically at the lines where the Devil brought the wife back as she was too much even for him in Hell.

There was a loud banging on the cell door. "Silence! Silence, mad Cavaliers."

Both men were laughing and crying at the same time.

"I had hoped that Katherine and I would have the same pattern to our marriage as yourself and Lady Howard." Richard watched his father in law as he ran his hands over his face to take away the tears.

"Do not wish that Richard." He said softly.

"But you are such good friends, I always feel great love when I visit your household. All is calm and happy, Katherine is always happy there."

"Yes, I love my wife, but not how a man should love a woman." He smiled, "We laugh together, she is my best friend, she is better to me than I deserve, for I have not been a good husband to her."

Lord Howard stood up to look out of the black metal bars over the open window. The warm fragrance of bread being baked and the smoke of wood fires were starting to rise with the sun. He sighed, "I am ashamed of myself Richard for the way I have treated Anne over the years. Had we been allowed to marry when we first met, perhaps it would have been different, but it was not to be"

Richard watched his father in law lean his chin on his crossed arms as he looked out of the window watching the town come to life. An early morning breeze lifted his tawny curled hair from his face as he thought. He looked into the waking town, listening to the cock crow, the dogs barking. Signs of life, normal life.

"I'm to go to God today, father. I am of no use to mine captors. So tell me for it will not leave my lips." Richard stood up and leant against the wall facing him.

"Katherine is our only child because I have the Black Lion." He sighed, "I gambled and whored while dear Anne kept me solvent, sane, and loved me." He pulled his fine lace collar down to show the seeping black stain of syphilis on his neck. "I could not in all good faith give this to her to suffer."

He pulled his collar back quickly to cover his shame. He watched the bright pretty milkmaids collect their empty wooden pails and yokes to walk to the fields. The cows were waiting patiently to be relieved of their full udders. It was a misty morning looking to become hot when the sun was high.

Lord Howard did not tell Richard that he caught the Black Lion from the many pretty boys he had paid to satisfy him. It was the only release from the deep melancholy he had felt all his life. It was called the Black Dog. Black, black like his life. He was black in heart and head, yet today he felt lighter, for he knew what he was going to do. He felt pleased that it didn't involve being tortured for information, or being ransomed back to his pretty wife to torment her.

Suddenly there was a loud bang on the cell door as it was thrown open. Two Guards stood side by side halberds in hand, one shouted gruffly. "Lord Richard Boyons? Come with us."

Lord Howard pushed Richard aside and moved forward. He took off his scabbard, doublet and felt hat. He threw them towards Richard and strode towards the men.

"Whatever else I am. I am no coward, Lord Howard." He smiled and winked at Richard as he was escorted out.

They walked across the courtyard towards the door of the church, old, once sturdy, now crumbling under the weight of the musket balls that had been aimed at it.

Lord Howard stood square on, smiling at the musketeers loading their guns. He waved away a blindfold.

Richard, on tip toes, craned his neck to see out of the window of his cell but could not see the church door.

He heard the orders being shouted. "Take aim, prepare to give fire, – FIRE!"

The sickening crack of the muskets echoed round the churchyard.

Lord Howard was still smiling. He was free, free of the blackness that had enveloped him in life, dying happily, as he watched the swallows swoop and circle in the clear blue sky above. He took his last breath in the warm dawn of a bright new summer's day.

The musketeers were re-loading ready for their next execution. A lieutenant came over to the body, looked into the smiling face, turned to the firing squad to shout. "What in Heavens name have you done? You imbeciles, you have murdered Lord Howard."

Richard Boyons had the unusual good luck to find himself a free man. Wearing Lord Howard's doublet, hat and empty scabbard at his side, he walked out of prison into the morning sunshine shielding his face with his hand.

He knew he was of no worth. He, unlike Lord Howard, had no knowledge of troop movements, there was no money or goods left for ransom for him. It had already been taken in the raid on the Boyons' manor. So all he was, was an extra mouth to feed, and a Cavalier mouth at that.

The road from Naseby to Leicester had been littered with the dead, mainly Royalist soldiers, killed as they became cumbersome. New Model Army miscreants who had been looting without permission, found themselves hanging from trees along the road, like some kind of ghastly decoration.

Desecrated Leicester smelt of death, and yet underneath the horror, there was some normality starting to appear.

Lord Howard, by his own happy sacrifice, had given Richard Boyons his life back. The commanding officer had decided not to tell of the mistake, he did not want to join the garlands of newly rotting corpses decorating the trees of the town. The men, he knew, would keep the secret to save their own skins. So Lord Richard Boyons had to go, not killed in case he was recognised. The door of his cell was unlocked, the guards turned their backs and he walked out a free man.

He wandered the dusty streets, stopping to look over the bridge of the River Stour to wonder what he should do next. He walked past an Inn at the side of the road, where the previous night, drunken celebrations of the victory turned into a fist fight over plunder. He kicked something in the dust, bent to pick it up to see what it was. A gold crown, then a ducket lay shining in the dirt, he kicked about innocently as if waiting for a friend, two more gold crowns turned up under his feet.

"Thank you God." He whispered to himself, looking up into the clear blue sky where the summer swallows were reeling and diving through the clouds.

He turned the coins over in his hands, "Thank you Howard, you have changed my luck." He decided not to push that luck by more kicking about in the dust.

He had enough now to go buy a horse and a sword. He would go home to see what was left of Boyons' manor and visit his tight mouthed mother who he was sure was still alive.

He walked through the resting Parliament Army, his head held high, unrecognised as a Royalist. For what Royalist would be mad enough to walk through a town taken by Parliament?

From a small garrison of soldiers at the side of the road he heard unnerving shouts of "An officer, salute boys!"

The soldiers who had been leaning on walls, drinking and laughing, dropped their breeches to show their filthy arses to him.

He ignored them and walked on, raucous laughter followed him down the street. Suddenly, silence and respect. A tall handsome man in blacked armour, with long black curled hair over his shoulders, saluted Richard by pulling his felt hat off. Thomas Fairfax, the Lord General of the Parliament Army stopped his magnificent white stallion to talk to him. He had two outriders to carry his baggage in straw baskets on either side of their less noble steeds.

"Where is your sword man? You are unarmed."

Richard took Lord Howard's black felt hat off as he swept into a bow. "Broken on Naseby field pulling it out of a rebel Sir."

"I recognise you do I not?" Fairfax's horse bridled and he pulled it to, "What's your name?"

"I can only remember Richard." Richard Boyons lied watching Lord Fairfax's face. Fairfax seemed to be trying to remember where he had seen this young man before.

"Here take this." He reached over to one of the straw baskets of his outriders, pulled out a sword and threw it to Richard who caught it neatly.

"Well caught." Fairfax grinned, assured now that this young man was well born, and been trained in sword school as he had. "You will need it for we move on the morrow."

"Where is your horse stabled?" Fairfax asked watching the rowdy soldiers by the inn out of the corner of his eye.

"I'm off to buy another, mine was shot from under me." That part was true, it was how he'd been captured with his colours. He swept a low bow in goodbye.

"Hold fast." Fairfax snapped.

Richard's heart near stopped. He turned to face the Lord General.

Fairfax took a folded piece of parchment from his bag. "A requisition for a horse," he smiled, "We cannot have our officers looking so poor that our men make fun of them."

He snapped his horse's reins to move on, and without looking back at the relieved Richard, Black Tom moved to bark orders at the soldiers who had laughed at him.

As he walked down the street Richard was starting to feel light of heart. Be careful, he told himself, be Puritan, be Roundhead. He saw a forge where two New Model Army soldiers were waiting to have repairs made to their halberds. One was a sergeant aged about forty, he was distinguished by the orange sash worn around his waist. He was stout and looked a decent sort of man.

"Sergeant, I am to requisition a horse." Richard showed him Fairfax's paperwork.

The man read it and handed it back to him. "This is for the Baggage Master, he'll provide one for you." He said brusquely knocking his pipe out on the side of the forge door. "Where is your officer's sash?"

"I lost all on Naseby field, my horse shot from under me, I was knocked out, when I awoke I had been looted. I do not even remember where I was taken or where the Baggage train is now, I've been wandering like a lost soul in purgatory until I met the Lord General who recognised me."

"Do you know your name?" The sergeant was interested now.

"I do not. Lord Fairfax called me Richard, so I suppose he must be right." The young man had a careworn honest face. He had bruises and cuts enough to prove he had fought hard.

"The Baggage is over the bridge, the horses are tied to a rope that runs along the road, they are guarded by a simpleton called Abe. Can't miss him." He pointed down the road with the stem of his pipe.

"Thank 'ee sergeant for your goodwill." Richard walked on in the direction of the Baggage train.

The sergeant's companion, a thin wiry man, came out from the forge with his newly mended halberd to dip it, hissing, into the barrel of water next to the door.

"Poor lad, sometimes it comes back, sometimes it don't." He watched Richard make his way down the street, "Praise be to God it does for him." He took his clay pipe, filled it, lit it and sucked hard to get the flavour.

“Has you seen it before Sarge?” the wiry man asked as he sharpened his halberd blade with his flint.

“Aye lad, in the Low Countries. I'm a professional soldier, I've fought, I've killed, I've seen much, but God knows it doesn't bother me.” He sighed, “but these young lads brought up high, merchants or brewers sons mayhap, thrown into the blood and thunder. Well it do block their minds.” He puffed on his pipe. “I've seen it afore, what be he eighteen or less?”

Richard Boyons' mind however was not blocked. Despite his father in law's sacrifice, he had started to feel hopeful. The men that fought each other on Naseby Field were not so very different from each other. Brother fought brother and son fought father, such was the schism in the land they both lived in. Both sides believing they were right and God was with them.

As these thoughts filled Richard Boyons' mind he became aware of a physical need. His stomach was rumbling. He walked along to a bakers shop, it was busy, so he waited his turn to buy a small loaf with his stomach making sounds like a small bear growling, enough to make other customers turn round and look.

“When did you last eat boy?” The baker's wife, a short, round woman with a clean apron and coif covering her hair watched his face for an answer.

“Two days since.” He replied truthfully.

“I have a little cheese and a few gobbets of bacon to hand for two pence.” She raced round towards him as he took out his leather pouch and removed the ducket. The gold glinted in the sun. As soon as she saw it, the baker's wife hoped to make more money from this lad, “Have you got a flask? Let me fill it for you, I have some fine small beer.”

“I have lost all on the field, I found this ducket down the street by the inn, it's all I have.” Richard said watching her ruddy, avaricious face. Have you such I can buy cheaply?”

"I have this," she bustled away behind the counter. "Twas dropped by a soldier drunk in my shop." She brought out a fine leather flask with a cork plug.

"I can't afford that." he looked at her with hollow eyes, "if I buy that from you I won't be able to eat for the rest of the week."

She turned and went back behind the counter and filled the flask with small beer. That's it, he thought, she will sell it full and make more money. Mayhap she will let me drink from her pewter mug for a penny to wash the bread down.

He found a corner with a milking stool. He sat on it, biting his bread. She bustled over. "Here we are my dear," She handed him the flask. He looked at her with puzzled eyes. "You dropped this in my shop yesterday." She winked at his tired, battle worn face.

After a week of cruelty and murder such kindness threw him. "Pay for the beer." she smiled and sat on the window seat beside him holding out her palm. He took a few more pence and dropped it into her floury, calloused hand. She rushed away and brought him a few gobbets of fried bacon and a small chunk of cheese wrapped in a small piece of linen.

As the salty flavours of the bacon burst into his mouth Richard's mouth began to water, he reached for the beer to take a long draught. He wiped the spittle away from his mouth with the back of his hand. "Will your husband beat you for showing me such kindness?" He asked watching her round motherly face.

"Lord preserve us no, I married a good man, we married for love. Hand-fasted at Harvest and married in Church at Christmas, fifteen years since." She seemed to like to gossip. "Are you married?"

"I am told my wife is dead," Richard said softly, "we were married but a twelve month."

"Dear Lord bless you, was it child bed?" The bakers wife asked.

"Soldiers." He stopped eating. "I cannot talk of it."

"Speak no more of it. Eat up, get your strength young man." She stood up to bustle away. "The shop is getting busy, I must work, God be with you."

"And you." Richard smiled. He had thought he had been having a good day until he remembered Katherine. It was not that he had forgotten about her, it was just that she had always been there since they were children together, he expected her always to be there.

He had thought eating and drinking would make him feel better, it didn't. It made him feel sick. He put the leftovers back in the linen, wrapped them up and tucked them inside his doublet.

As he walked out of the warm shop he felt a cool breeze rise, he held his father in law's felt hat in place with his hand to stop it blowing away. There was a smell of death in the air. Smoke from the blacksmiths and bakers did not hide the putrid smell of rotting flesh pervading the town. He walked towards the fields where the Baggage Train had camped. He wandered through the rows of tents towards the tethered horses, wondering whether his luck would hold.

The Cherry Tree Inn,
Market Harborough, 18th June 1645

A woman is like chaff blown in the wind. Owned by men, directed by men. She moves from one to another to keep herself from harm; from blowing away completely, never to be seen again.

I knew Rupert by reputation. As a Lady of Quality and the only one within his reach, I knew how I had to pay for my bed and keep that night. I prepared myself by inserting a small sheep's bladder into my cunny. I took charge to make sure his dogge visited it properly, then threw away any disease he might have given me out of the window into the dusty street below.

I did not love Rupert, I obliged him. I felt nothing as he took me, my experience of men had taught me how to make him end quickly, and so it was.

I had heard that when asked why he did not marry any of the mothers of his daughters, (he seemed unable to beget a son), he had replied.

"When one treads in a cowpat, one then does not wear it on his head for all to see." He was arrogant, selfish and manipulating, I hoped to be free of him.

I was lying in bed collecting my thoughts when I heard drums beating 'Make Ready' in the street. I could hear the clatter of armour and boots as soldiers ran to their ranks. I quickly put on a clean shift and front lacing stays which did not need help from a maid. I was feeling sick with panic as I got ready to leave.

There was a loud persistent knock on the door. Rupert had long gone from me, staggering back to Maurice's room before sunrise. I was alone gathering my clothes and thoughts together.

Jonathan shouted through the door. "Lady Anne, Lady Howard, the King wishes to see you urgently." He was almost inaudible because of the noise of the Regiments forming up in the street below.

"One moment, one moment," I shouted back hurriedly fastening my linen skirt and fustian bodice. I slipped on my hose tying them above the knee tightly, then put my shoes on. I looked in the mirror, was I fit to see the King?

I quickly put a kerchief around my neck to cover the red marks Rupert had made there. "Marked by love," he had laughed. I frowned, I felt like a despoiled milkmaid.

"Madam," Jonathan begged through the door, "make haste. I will take your bags for you."

I rushed along to the Kings rooms and knocked on the door. It was opened by a young man I had not seen in the King's entourage before.

"Your Majesty," I curtseyed low, "You wished to see me."

He put his finger across his lips as he had always done to stop a stutter. He looked tired, he had been up all night writing letters, his fingers were ink stained and a candle had burnt out on the table where he had been working.

"We have news Lady Howard." His lips worked, trying to control his stutter. "This morn, by this young messenger, he is a good man and will tell you all."

The young man who had opened the door for me stepped forward. "I have ridden hard to get here before the King departed." He was about nineteen, had an unremarkable face. A face that could be lost in a crowd, a face like many others. I understood immediately why he was chosen as a spy for the

King. His buff coat was dusty from the road. Sweating and tired, he none the less swept an elegant bow in front of me.

My heart thumped uncontrollably, this was to be bad news.

"Your Ladyship, your husband Lord Howard was killed by musket shot at dawn this morning, mistaken for another prisoner."

"My husband you say?" I dropped onto the floor in shock and started to sob. "Is this really true? If it is, then I have indeed lost all."

"He should have been tortured and ransomed, but he exchanged doublets with another prisoner. He died in his place." The young man looked across at the King. "He told them nothing your Majesty."

The King nodded sagely. I noticed Prince Rupert, majestically dressed, standing by the King. He was watching me, smiling, then covered his smile with his hand. He leant over and whispered in the Kings ear. Charles smiled. "Not yet sir, let the dust settle." He whispered to his nephew.

"It was a brave sacrifice." I sobbed for my husband, my best friend. He had been cuckolded by two of the men standing in this room. If he had have known he would have understood. He had never been faithful to me.

"What now?" I pulled myself up to stand, holding the back of a chair. "To what is left of my Manor I suppose." I was shaking, Jonathan moved forward to support my elbow to help me out of the room.

Prince Rupert nudged King Charles' elbow. "We think that you will need protection dear lady, my nephew here has recommended Lord Dunbar for the job. You are part Scots after all, it would be like returning home."

"You are too kind." I choked out, "But it is too soon Your Majesty." I curtseyed and walked backwards out of the room.

The Baggage Train, Leicester, 16th June 1645

Katherine was about her business as Doctor John Bastwick's new 'boy'. She felt she would not be under his protection for too much longer as he had told her that he didn't have the stomach for another battle. He had been making preparations to leave almost as soon as the Baggage Train had set up camp.

"Why are you leaving? Where will you go?" She asked gruffly, her throat still sore.

He pulled off his wig and put it in it's box, ready to be packed into the back of his wagon.

"I'm going home to my wife and children," he smiled sadly at her. "I must, for who will protect them if not me?"

"Take me with you." She pleaded with tears in her eyes.

"You know I cannot, you do not belong with me." He started loading the boxes. "You must go home."

"How can I go home? Dressed like this, I shall be thought a deserter should I try to leave now." She closed a box of medicines and handed them to him.

"I have written you a pass." He smiled handing her a parchment with a wax seal. "It is in the name of K. Carpenter, tis up to you how you wish to appear. Will that do?"

She took the parchment and read it. "Twill do, can I not travel with you just as far as Market Harborough? My home is not far from there."

"My dear, my home is in Wales, I have a small farm hidden away in the valley. I will go there. Where in due time I will die peacefully with my family around me, having lived a quiet life in my declining years." He climbed onto the wagon, slapped the reins across the horses back, and started to move off. "I am tired, fifty years old now. War is no place for an old man." He looked round at her, "I have left you something of use in the box under your bed." He waved goodbye without looking back.

"Thank you." Katherine's hoarse voice called after him. "Thank you Doctor."

She watched his wagon until it disappeared over the bridge, tears started to fall, she wiped them away with her grubby hand.

Alone, she thought, after two days of kindness from the Doctor, I must fend for myself. She had got herself this far, she was still alive, she still had hope.

In the Doctor's tent he had left her camp bed and blankets, and hidden underneath was a black leather box out of sight of any curious soldier who may have looked in.

How empty it seems, she thought. He had taken the floor coverings of rough linen, the sheepskins and his tapestries from the walls. Her carpet was now bright green grass and dried cowpats. She pulled the box out to look inside it.

Katherine didn't expect to see much, but he had done his best for her. A cleanish shift for a woman, a brown linen skirt, a green bodice, a coif embroidered with blackwork. She tried not to imagine the woman's dead body he had taken it off. There was a small leather pouch with two pence in it, enough for a piece of bread. She decided to change back to her own sex. As she did so she gently peeled the plaister from the cut on on her inner thigh. It came off easily but pinched the skin. The cut had mended and it was healing well. She tried to peel the plaister off her right thigh. As she picked at the corner, a disgusting smell of rotting flesh assailed her nose. The wound was open, looked worse, the skin around it black and rancid.

She quickly poured some lavender oil on a rag and tied it around her wound. Panic was rising in her throat. It didn't hurt, she could feel nothing, she had seen this before. It was gangrene.

"God's will be done." She whispered hoarsely time and again. She walked out into the warm day, sweating with fear. She took out her pass and read it.

'K. Carpenter, doctor's assistant. Free pass as far as Oxford to buy apothecary supplies for New Model Army, by order of Doctor John Bastwick.' It was signed and sealed with red wax. She rolled it and put it in the leather pouch with the coins.

Taking a deep breath, she lifted her head high and strode across the field to where the horses had been stabled. She walked towards the simple boy who was in charge of the row of horses to show him her pass to see if it would entitle her to a horse. He gangled towards her, ungainly, grinning. He couldn't read, so she showed him the red wax seal, he recognised it by running his fingers over it. She then told him it was a pass to travel to Oxford and a request for a horse. He looked at her wondering what business she was about, he asked her that question.

"I'm from the Baggage, I'm to go and fetch medicines from the Apothecary." She looked him up and down smiling sweetly. "Surely a young man with an important job such as yours recognises Dr Bastwick's assistant?"

He didn't, but flattered by her attentions said he did. "You'm alone?" He asked hopefully looking her up and down, licking his lips. He handed her back the pass.

Suspecting what the rough young man had in mind Katherine lied. "No, here comes my husband now." She saw a tall, well dressed man coming towards them.

The young man squeezed his eyes against the sun. "Aww. The good 'uns are always taken." He said slightly annoyed. "Take any one of them." He pointed to a row of skittish and kicking horses.

Katherine watched the well dressed young man approaching her, he too was carrying a pass, but his had Fairfax's seal. He stared at the poorly dressed young woman, she looked familiar.

She stared back at him, looking at a man she thought may have been a stranger, or who may have been dead. She kept her countenance, not wanting to give anything away, but she had butterflies in her stomach as he grew closer to her.

Richard's heart leapt. Could this be true? He walked coolly towards her, pulled her close and kissed her on the lips. "Katherine," he breathed softly, "Is it really you?"

"Richard," she held him tight, "God's teeth Richard, I thought I'd never see you again."

"Do not swear madam," he scolded gently, "I have not the money for fines."

The boy giggled, embarrassed, hopping from one foot to the other, "I'll not tell, hee, hee, God's teeth, that's a good one!"

"Husband and wife, proper, I'll wager." He laughed, watching them embracing. "Here, take this for your trouble and give us two good horses." Richard gave the boy a groat, the boy bit it and whistled through his teeth on finding it real. "You can have one good one!" He grinned. He untied a large bay stallion that had been snorting and stamping and throwing his head back to whinny as loud as he could. His big brown eyes had recognised his master and mistress. "You can have him, no one else can ride him, we found him cropping grass on the Kineton road." The boy shambled off towards the inn to spend his money.

"Balthazar!" Katherine and Richard said together. The stallion's eyes widened as he snuzzled into Katherine's hands. They walked him out into the lane.

"Oh my Richard, I'm so glad I've found you." She hung on his arm, "I've so much to tell you." Her voice was still gruff but getting better, lighter, along with her spirits. "I think I am going to die, I am so glad you will be with me, I can bear anything if you are near."

Richard stopped in his tracks. "What makes you think you are going to die?" he asked, stunned. "I've only just found you, I won't let you go now."

They sat on a fallen tree by the side of the road, and she explained to him about the cuts on her legs.

He listened patiently, desperately wanting to tell her of the brave sacrifice her father had made for him. His mind was clouded with all the death he had seen on the road to this dusty, dirty little town, full of tanneries and forges. "Katherine did he rape you – this soldier?" He took her hands in his.

"No, he tried and failed. Balthazar reared on his back and trampled him underfoot." She looked into her husband's clear blue eyes. "I did something awful. I killed him. I stabbed his chest, then slit his throat, as he had tried to slit mine." She pulled her linen collar from her neck to show him, livid red blood spots lay on the mending wound. "I'm a murderer."

Richard took a deep breath. "I understand wife, it was kill or be killed, tis the nature of war, God will forgive you." He put his hand into hers. "The Lord will understand."

"I did something worse." She started to shake.

"You can tell me." He drew her close to comfort her.

"I was angry, so very angry Richard." She looked up into his kind face. "What I did was very bad," she took a breath, "I cut his penis off."

Richard laughed in shock.

"Tis amusing?" She was tearful and shaking. "You are laughing at me?"

"Love, he cannot go to heaven or be resurrected now, only those complete in body and soul can do so." He held her to him tightly to reassure her.

"What will happen to me?" She asked. "At my time of reckoning?" She held him tightly making his ribs ache where the musket stocks of his captors had paid their attentions.

"You will be saved my love, our God loves us," he smiled, "loves you."

"I want to go home to mother, she will know what to do." She implored him. "Please."

"My love, we need a Cunning Woman quickly, the rot you speak of moves speedily." He lifted her onto Balthazar's broad back and pulled himself up behind her.

"I know, I have been but two days helping the Doctor and I have already seen how fast it works. I'm scared Richard."

They rode back towards the town with Richard racking his brains to find someone who could help. He headed towards the Blacksmith where he had met the sergeant.

Katherine had given him the Doctor's orange sash, he wore it diagonally across his chest from his shoulder to his waist, marking him out as a Parliament Officer. She had taken it from under the bed where he had hidden it before he deserted.

Richard arrived at the forge to be disappointed. The sergeant and his companion had left some time ago. He slid off Balthazar's broad back to walk in and speak to the Blacksmith.

"Ho sir, where has the sergeant gone?"

The Smith looked up at him. "To the Inn." He grunted hammering a horse shoe, red hot from the fire.

"I have found my wife alive with the baggage," Richard explained, "but she is mortal wounded with a festering cut. I have need to see a Cunning woman. Do you know of one?"

The Blacksmith stood up, taller and broader than Richard, sweating and covered in ash from the fire. His eyes glinted as he weighed up the young man before him. "My wife is a Goodwyfe she knows many remedies, but times are hard, do you have gold coins in that purse on your belt?" He eyed up the leather pouch hanging at Richard's side.

The hair on Richard's neck stood up in warning, he felt he could not trust this man. "I have been looted on the field, I have nothing in my pouch."

"Then we cannot help you." The Smith immediately lost interest. He turned to drench the red hot horseshoe he had been hammering in a barrel of cold water where it steamed and hissed.

Richard walked out into the hot sun, to Katherine waiting patiently on Balthazar's back. Using the mounting stone he got onto the horse in front of her.

"Where are we going?" She asked worried.

"To the Inn, that man is not to be trusted." He answered clicking his tongue to move the stallion on.

"Is that where the Parliament soldiers are?" She held his waist tightly. "I don't like this."

"You know as well as I do dear heart, that they are just men like us." As their horse moved forwards through the hot busy town, Richard suddenly had an idea. "The Baker's wife, she will know what to do."

He stopped in front of the shop, it had closed, it being past noon. All the bread had been sold in the morning, the dough was being kneaded and proved for the next bake at the back of the shop. They could hear the baker and his wife laughing together as they chatted and worked.

Richard slid off Balthazar's back and walked round to the side door of the shop, overlooking a small pretty garden. He hammered on the door.

"Hold on, hold on," came a shout from the back. May opened the door, her hands and face covered in flour. "Oh it's you! - You've come up in the world," she smiled looking at the orange sash.

"With so many men dead, those left living are given privileges they don't deserve." He said quickly. "I have found my wife, but she is mortal sick, she needs a Cunning woman or some such." His eyes implored her. "You are a kind woman, please can you help? Do you know of anyone in the town?"

May looked up at the pale willowy young woman on the horse's back. "Dusty my lover," she called to her husband, "I'll be back in a moment."

Richard lifted Katherine gently down from the horse. Both ladies curtseyed to each other.

"Mistress, how can I help?" May could see no obvious wound, so she imagined it was in the private parts. "My name is May Miller," she smiled, "come sit in my garden to talk privy."

They walked to an old millstone, now a garden seat, they whispered together for a few moments while Richard impatiently held a hot and restless Balthazar.

"Mistress Miller will help, her sister is a Goodwyfe, better than any cunning woman she tells me." Katherine held Richards arm, "I feel hopeful." she smiled.

"She's but a few doors away." May rushed down the street to her sister's house leaving clouds of flour in her wake. She waved from the doorstep for Richard and Katherine to follow.

Where Mistress May Miller was rosy cheeked, round and merry. Her sister, an old maid, was tall, thin and serious. Precise in her dress, neat and clean. Katherine liked her immediately. She felt confident this woman would know what she was doing.

"Come with me." She snapped at Katherine. "You..." she pointed at Richard, "take that horse to the water trough at the end of my garden, he looks over hot and needs a drink."

"Thank you Goodwyfe." Richard watched puzzled as Katherine followed May's sister to the cool of the dairy at the back of the house.

May slapped Richard on the shoulder with a floury hand. "She's a dry old stick, none would know she's my sister," she laughed, "but she knows what she's doing."

"How can I thank you?" Richard asked smiling feintly.

"Show me your children, come back when this cursed war is over, and let them play in my garden and make me laugh." She raced off back down the street to the bakery. "I must go, the bread will not knead itself in time for the morrow!" She waved a floury hand as she disappeared into her garden.

Richard led the horse to the trough, and as the great bay slurped noisily at the water, he sat on the edge of the trough, amazed at the kindness of people in such dire times.

In the cool dark dairy, Katherine was asked to sit on a settle by the open door to the herb garden where the light was better. Savoury, lavender, rue and bright yellow heads of tansy bobbed in the warm breeze. Apples and pears were starting to take shape amongst the blossom on the trees. A large ginger cat snored nosily on the path.

"I am Mistress Felicity Vasey." She took Katherine's hot dusty hand in her cool clean one. "You are?"

"Katherine Carpenter," she lied. She did not after all, know what this woman's political leanings were, and she needed to be treated.

"Show me the problem." She said coldly and efficiently.

Katherine explained how the wounds came about as she lifted her skirts and shifts, hiding her cunny with her hand and part of her shift.

Felicity's clean cold hands peeled back the lavender soaked bandage Katherine had applied to herself. "Ah, Mistress you have tried, but lavender is no good in this case."

The stain of gangrene had grown larger, and the stench stuck in both their throats as the bandage was removed.

"I am a clean woman," Katherine blurted out, " I truly am, I am so sorry."

"I will not fool you child, this will not be easy to treat, but I think I can do it. Does your husband have money?" she asked covering the wound with a dry piece of clean linen.

"I think we can pay you." Katherine said urgently.

"No, not for me my dear," Felicity's thin mouth moved into a kind smile. "I do not want your money. We will need to buy laudanum and plaister from the Apothecary."

Katherine smiled. "Thank you."

"Do not thank me yet you are not cured, but at least you will not feel my ministrations." Felicity went to Richard standing by his horse to give him directions and a shopping list for the Apothecary."

He strode down the street on his mission with a heavy heart. Meanwhile Katherine was laying back on the settle while Felicity applied maggots to the wound to clear it out. As they filled themselves with the poison, they dropped off sated. Felicity picked them off the cold stone floor to return them to their box containing a small piece of pig fat and closed the lid.

"Can you feel anything yet?" The Goodwyfe asked as she washed her hands under the pump.

"Yes, yes, I feel pain." Katherine screamed out. "Dear God, help me, make it stop, make it stop."

Felicity gave a stern little smile. "You may not think so, but that is a good thing, my disgusting little friends have done their job well."

Richard burst into the dairy holding out a green bottle to Felicity. "Laudanum."

She took the bottle and put four drops directly onto Katherine's tongue and washed it down with cold clean water taken from the well in her garden.

"I'm glad you are back. You will need to hold her still while I do my work." She watched Richard's face. "Can you do that?"

She came from her Kitchen with a large sharp knife she had been heating on the stove.

Luckily, Katherine had passed out. The laudanum had done it's work.

As she was about to put the hot knife to Katherine's thigh she looked up at Richard. "This will mark, it will not be pretty, but she will live, does that bother you?" She watched his concerned face.

"No." Richard held his wife down, so that Felicity could do her work. "She is my wife, my love, it will not put me off her, if that's what you think."

"Good man." Felicity smiled her tight little smile as she cut carefully round the heavily bleeding wound. White hot, the knife sealed the cut as it removed the black debris. When the work was done she washed the wound with willow powder and lavender, applied a wet plaister and covered it with a linen bandage. She stood up sweating and shaking, went to the garden pump and washed her hands with the soft soap used for the laundry.

"She cannot move for at least three days." She came back into the dairy, drying her hands. "I have a good room here, and it means I can look after her." She looked at Richard. "The gossip round the town is that the New Model Army are to move off tomorrow. Richard took of his sash and folded it into his hand. "They do not need me, she does."

"You will be executed as a deserter." Felicity's eyes watched his tired and battle worn face.

"Either way I will die." He stood up to walk along the street. "I will go and see if I can be given furlough, join them later." He lied as he headed for the Inn to drink a well deserved beer.

The Cherry Tree Inn,

Market Harborough, 19th June 1645

I was standing in the King's rooms, around him new bags and boxes were being packed, his Colonels and Men at Arms waiting patiently for orders. He had rolled up the last of his letters, put a seal on it from his signet ring then looked up at me.

I was distraught, I had lost my husband, my daughter. I desperately wanted to go back to my Manor.

"You must go to Leicester, to Cromwell, ask to see your husband, petition for his release." The King stuttered. "He does not know he is dead."

"What good will that do your Majesty?" I asked him red eyed. "I want to go home, in two days I could be there, seeing to my affairs."

"If Cromwell finds out what has happened, that he has lost Lord Howard and the information he holds and the gold he is worth... Well madam, I should like to be a fly on that wall." He was offered his doublet by his valet, he put it on. "I am sure he will offer you something of worth, perhaps an amnesty on your Manor." He offered his sleeves to be buttoned up. "If not, you will certainly find something of use to me. Learn all you can."

"So I am to be a spy again?" I sighed and wiped my eyes.

"You are playing a part." Rupert smiled at me. "You are after all, rather good at it."

He knew my tricks, of course he did, an experienced young man like him.

"Find out all you can." The King picked up his cane and hat. "Meet me at Raglan Castle, I am in need of respite. My dear bold nephew is for Bristol."

"I may be for Bristol, but I will send for Lord Dunbar to come and offer you his protection." Rupert smiled, he was playing with me, knowing I had not the stomach for such a liaison.

"Please do not." I sighed, "Your Majesty, Charles," I pleaded, "let me to my Manor, I have not the coin for such a journey."

Rupert threw me his money pouch. "Take it, it's all we have." He grinned at me. "You cannot disobey an order from your King."

Leicester, 19th June 1645

We set off for Leicester at the King's command, by the time we had arrived, Cromwell and Fairfax had moved on. It was a dirty, busy little town, full of tanneries, forges and stables. The aftermath of an Army invasion was devastating, many badly wounded soldiers had been left behind and begged at the side of the road. It seemed the whole of the churchyard had been opened up and graves gaped like hungry children waiting to be fed. Ragged women railed and cried as they looked for their loved ones, and underneath all this was a town trying to go about it's business as if nothing had happened.

"We must go to the church, if Howard is there we will bring him to be buried at home." I sobbed. My best friend, my dear kind husband, lay in the piles of bodies waiting to be buried.

Jonathan walked to the old cleric in charge of the burials and explained who we were looking for. He looked across at me short-sightedly as he pointed to six bodies laying in a row under what used to be an army tent. Jonathan waved me over.

"These are the men of quality." The old cleric stumbled. "They were shot yesterday morn." He opened the door of the tent, it smelt like a charnel house on a warm day. Blood and worse.

I spotted him immediately, wearing the shirt with his Belgian lace collar that I had made him for his birthday. His eyes were still open, but dulled. He was smiling. I felt as if I had been punched in the chest by a pike. I stroked his tawny hair from his eyes as I closed them. I suddenly felt angry, really angry. He was pleased to leave, pleased to go to God and be forgiven.

"Howard." I choked out.

"What's to do Madam?" The old cleric's watery eyes looked at me. He held out his hand. "If you tell me your address, and give me a coin or two, I can have a carter take him home this afternoon, do you live far?"

"I have no money to take him home, bury him here in the churchyard, I will come to make arrangements when the war is over, so do not cheat me." I handed a few coins into the fragile curate's bony hand. "Tis enough," he said watching my face, "name?"

"Lord Howard". I took one last look at the face of the man who had shared my life and my bed for near on twenty years.

"I shall put it on a wooden cross, you may mark his grave properly after the war is over." The cleric said a small prayer, wrote something on a piece if parchment and lay it on Howard's chest, putting a small stone to hold it in place.

I walked away head down, holding Jonathan's arm tightly. "I am tired and it's getting late," he helped me back onto the horse. "We need to find lodgings."

We made our way to a stables halfway down the street. Jonathan led our horse to the water trough outside and went in to see if the stable hand could help in any way. I sat on the mounting stone with my throbbing head in my hands. I put my hand into the cold water and rubbed my hot forehead with my icy fingers. Cold, refreshing. Jonathan was back in a moment. "I have given the lad a few coins to feed and stable our horse tonight. He tells me of a Goodwyfe who may let us stay the night. I told him you were exhausted from travelling. I leant heavily on Jonathan's arm, with grief and tiredness starting to overcome me, we walked up the dusty darkening road to Mistress Vasey's house.

In the stables Richard was finishing his day's tasks. He fed the horses, the few that the New Model Army had not taken when they left, and was brushing the foaming sweat off the coat of the horse that had just been brought in. His few pieces of gold had not lasted long, the price of medicines being what they are during war time. His few gold pieces had been spent in just three days, the few coins he had left he had saved for the Church fines. He would go on Sunday of course, but Katherine would have to pay a fine as she could not attend the service as she was too ill.

He had offered himself to the owner of the stables, a young widowed woman, who was glad of the help for just enough money to pay for their food. It wasn't much but he could at least contribute to Goodwyfe Vasey for the kindness and care she had shown them.

Balthazar was not with the horses at the stables near the Smithy, he was happily cropping grass and fresh hay in a small field at the back of Felicity Vasey's house. A powerful stallion like him would have been stolen overnight on the first night if he'd been left in the stables in the town. He was out of sight of the road and locked away each evening in the stable behind the dairy with the cow and her calf.

As he walked back to his lodgings Richard was smiling, not long now and they would be back in the lush green fields of Oxfordshire. They had decided to go straight to Lady Howard's Manor and tell her all. Richard didn't relish seeing his mean tight faced mother immediately. He would have to work up to it. The sun was setting, making the air cooler as he walked the dusty streets. He was looking forward to having his second meal of the day, talking with Katherine, and hopefully seeing some progress in her recovery.

Mistress Vasey opened the door to Lady Howard and Jonathan, she showed them into her best room at the back of the house overlooking the garden.

"It will be one piece of gold, and you will have to save two shillings for the Church collection tomorrow." She said in her practical voice.

I collapsed onto a chair. "Madam we are Royalists, if you do not want us in your house I will understand. We do not have a gold piece, I have but ten shillings and nine pence." I poured the contents of my pouch onto the polished wooden table. "I have paid to bury my husband today, we have paid for stabling and feeding our horse, we have not eaten since yesterday evening, so take what you want. I no longer care."

She looked at me surprised. "Well, you are straight lady."

Jonathan was confused, was the Goodwyfe going to give us away?

She sat opposite me and took two shillings and sixpence, put the rest back into the pouch and gave it back to me. "I have some bread, bacon, herb and cheese soup."

"Here is the bed." She undid the sides of an old Knole sofa. She put cushions on the floor beside it. It looked to be a comfortable double bed although it was dusty. She bustled away and came back with clean white linen sheets and a tapestry coverlet.

In a moment she was back again with bread and soup, she put the green glazed pottery dishes on the table. Neither Jonathan nor I were looking forward to the meal, but it was delicious.

When Felicity came back to clear the table my eyes were closing with the warmth of the food and the comfort of the sofa. "We were a Royalist town, now we are Puritan," she picked up the pewter soup spoons and put them in the dishes. "Our lives change with the wind. I was always Royalist in my heart, but always puritan in my dress." She smiled and her stern face softened. "For my man was for Parliament, believing all men should be equal in the sight of God."

"Does he still fight for Cromwell?" Asked Jonathan.

"No, for the poor soul was killed in battle at Edgehill. The first battle of the war." She sighed. "We were to have been married on his return."

I looked up at her drowsily. "What will you do now?"

"I will sell herbs for cooking, and to the apothecaries. Let my good rooms to those travelling." She smiled, "I am finding I can do quite well without having the heartbreak of romance."

"I wish I could be my own woman." I looked at Jonathan. "But I cannot, my husband is dead but two or three days and I have already been espoused to a stranger."

"Can you not get out of it?" She asked watching my exhausted white face.

"No, for it has been settled by the King himself." I stifled a yawn.

"Sleep now, the bells will ring for Church at nine." She took the dishes to the door.

"We shall be gone before cock crow." Jonathan lounged in a chair by the window. "We have a way to travel tomorrow."

"As you wish. If you leave your flasks outside the door I will fill them for you."

Felicity shut the door behind her and we could hear her shoes clatter down the hallway to the kitchen. Jonathan took our leathern bottles and lay them on the tiles outside the door.

In a moment he was in bed beside me, lifting my shift and kissing my breasts. "I must have you." He whispered against my cheek. "My love, my woman."

So he did have me. I was as Shakespeare called it, caught in the land between waking and sleeping. He rose like the stars to fill me full of heaven's delight.

The following day, Sunday, Richard, Katherine and Goodwyfe Vasey made their way to St Leonard's Church. Katherine rode on the back of a small donkey borrowed from Dusty and May Miller. Her face grey and her legs sore, she was nonetheless determined to go. Firstly to save the fine money and secondly to see if she was well enough to travel.

The Church had largely been desecrated by the Puritan Soldiers. They had torn down the statues of the Saints, graven images they called them. The Church door had been used as a background against which to execute prisoners. The soldiers had stolen the plate and cups and cross from the altar, then brutally murdered the Vicar who tried to stand in their way.

Today four soldiers, two with halberds and two with muskets, watched the congregation to make sure they were all coming to pray.

Katherine limped to a pew at the back of the church. "Are you all right my love?" Richard whispered. She nodded.

An enthusiastic young man took to the pulpit, dressed entirely in black, he stood like a crow about to launch himself down and pick at the bones of the congregation.

He put his arms in the air. "Thanks be to God." He shouted. "Look about you citizens, see for yourself what we have done. There are no barriers to our Lord God. I shall now read you a commandment of the Parliament of our blessed land, written on the 8th of June to you, their people."

Complete silence in the church. Even the fear of breathing too hard also abounded.

He continued. "Listen and pay heed to what I say. For as much as the feast of the nativity of Christ, Easter, Whitsuntide, and other festivals, commonly called holy-days, have been heretofore superstitiously used and observed; be it ordained, that the said feasts, and all other festivals, commonly called holy-days, be no longer observed as festivals; any law, statute, custom, constitution, or canon, to the contrary in anywise notwithstanding." He smiled,

"Every day therefore is Christ's day – is that not good?"

Silence.

"We shall say the Lord's Prayer, followed by a prayer for Lord Fairfax and his mighty army and for our brave leader Lieutenant General Oliver Cromwell."

Afterwards as the congregation filed out, coins were dropped in the collecting boxes held by the soldiers. Katherine hobbled over to the newly dug graves. She sat on a small gravestone as she waited for Richard to bring the donkey around to her. Bored, she began to read the names of the deceased painted on the wooden crosses. "Colonel Robert Russell of Essex"

"Lord Howard of Oxfordshire".

Richard came across with the Miller's little donkey, he scooped Katherine up gently to put her on it's back. "Is that my father?" She whispered tearfully. "Why didn't you tell me?"

"Tace." he snapped at her.

"You sound just like your mother." Katherine said angrily.

"What's to do?" A soldier who had been loitering nearby asked.

"My wife is not well, in pain." Richard smiled.

"Probably her courses, get her with child as soon as maybe." The soldier laughed, showing crooked brown teeth from smoking too much tobacco. "Soon calm her down!"

Katherine bit her lip as tears fell.

On the journey back to their rooms, Richard told her of her father's brave sacrifice, and why he couldn't tell her, so ill as she was.

"I understand." She sobbed. "I think I can ride home now."

"I will look and see what is what, when we get to my house." Mistress Vasey smiled, "You are making good progress."

Katherine went straight up to her room and bed to rest. She gently peeled the plaister from her inner thigh. There was no smell, but there was blood. She called out for Felicity.

"Tis doing well, but such a small trip opened the wound. You must wait until it heals completely." Felicity put a dry linen patch over the wound. "A week or so."

Meeting Cromwell on the road to Bridgewater 1645

We waited and waited, we had petitioned the man by letter sent ahead by rider which cost us the last of our money. Eventually, I alone was shown into an elegant wood panelled room in a small Manor house. Feeling sick with fear I curtseyed to the man who had my husband shot.

He was not tall as his portraits showed him to be. He was of farming stock and it showed, scruffy, but well built with a bulbous red nose. One of his pretences was that he was related to Thomas Cromwell, Henry the Eighth's minister, but rumours throughout Royalist circles indicated that he had taken the name to advance himself.

"I have come to ask for my husband's freedom." I said boldly staring into his blue grey eyes. "I hear you take petitions from Ladies such as myself seriously."

He looked at some papers on the desk. "Lady Howard is it?" He smiled, "I took your husband into custody myself on Naseby field a few weeks ago."

"How is he?" I asked, knowing full well the answer.

"Still a coward, I suppose." He sneered. "What can you offer me? Your pretty daughter perhaps?"

"My daughter sir, was raped and killed at her home by one of your soldiers." He took a miniature from his pocket and slid it across the table to me. It was indeed Katherine. "I'm sorry to hear that Madam. I like the company of young women.

They are bright, ornamental, and sing prettily for me. I was hoping to meet her."

"She cannot sing with a cut throat." I started to sob. "How would you feel if your beloved Betty was forced to the floor, stripped, raped and had her throat cut?"

"Madam, you go too far. Your Cavaliers are as violent as any man on the field. If any man touched my daughter...." His rough hewn face flared red.

"They would not." I sobbed, "my Cavaliers would not..."

I could see by his infuriated face he did not agree.

"Let us not lose the point of this meeting." He said kindly as he sat down. "Please sit, I am a reasonable man."

"My husband is not perfect, but he is my best friend, what do you want from me to release him?" I dried my eyes with my kerchief. I had dressed in the best plain clothes I could find, I wanted him to take me seriously.

Outside the room Jonathan was talking to the guards as he waited. I was not the only woman waiting to see the Lieutenant General. There were many more sitting in the corridor of the Manor fiddling with their bags and kerchiefs waiting to pay their ransoms.

"Does he ever take anything in kind?" Jonathan asked cheekily.

"Not from these women, he likes young girls rising fifteen or so." The guard laughed. "He dandles them on his knee and they sing to him."

"Quiet." The older guard snapped. "Tis none of our business. He does the same to his own daughter Elizabeth, he misses being a father – that's all."

The other soldier winked at Jonathan in a way that made him shudder.

I looked up at the Lord General, hoping to bargain with him. I knew it was futile. I knew I had already lost everything that had meant anything to me.

Cromwell however, did not.

"When I left my home I had four good horses, a small herd of cows, some sheep, many good fat hens and geese."

Cromwell roared with laughter. "Wars are not fought with poultry madam, what of your arms, powder, cannon, gold?"

"I have none. Howard was a gambler, there was no gold. When we had any money I bought for the farm so at least we would not starve." I turned the painting of Katherine over in my fingers looking at her pretty blonde curls, perfectly shaped full mouth, and the twinkle in her eyes.

I felt sick.

"That I can understand." He smiled kindly. "Life has not been good to you has it? It will all change, when God sits with us in Parliament it will all change."

He hammered on the door. "Guard bring Lord Howard to me. As a show of kindness to a Lady in distress, I will take your Manor, servants and livestock as the ransom and give you back your daughter's portrait as a sign of good faith."

My own property, the miniature of my daughter, I thought to myself, he gives me back my own property as a gift.

"Where did you get the portrait from if I may ask?" I looked across at him.

He laughed. "A Cavalier boy taken to be ransomed, but as it turns out we had already taken payment from his Manor."

"What happened to him?" It was Richard, I knew it was.

"Shot." The Lieutenant General answered shortly. "We do not keep extra mouths to feed while we are on the march."

I heard a scuffle outside as the Guard raced off to find my husband.

About five awkward minutes later, a nervous Sergeant at arms appeared. He was pushed into the room by the two guards. "Tell him." They commanded.

"Lord Howard was shot by accident in Leicester" he blurted out. "Before we could question him. The musketeers had mixed him up with another prisoner who was worthless."

Cromwell took his pistol from the table in front of him, cocked it, and shot the Sergeant dead in front of me. The guards dragged him out.

I sat in the chair, shocked, while Cromwell wrote and signed a document for me. "I am more sorry than I can say, this is a dreadful war," he handed me the note. "Your Manor will not be touched in any way detrimental madam, I give you my word."

I took the parchment he had signed and sealed, I was stunned at his efficiency.

"Next..." Cromwell shouted.

The King in Raglan Castle, July 1645

We made our way to Raglan and arrived dusty and dirty from the roads. I was feeling my age, my stays hurt from rubbing my ribs while riding, I was overly hot and very hungry. My legs ached from the constant jogging of our poor horse's trotting. Tears of tiredness burned my eyes.

"I am too old to do this. Everything hurts." I said to Jonathan. He seemed a little more cheerful than I, having reached bed and board after days of riding.

"I am but fifteen years younger madam, I ache too, this poor creature is too bony to ride for long distances." He turned our almost dead horse towards the gate.

We both got off. The poor animal had travelled too many miles, no Inn or stables we stopped at could give us exchange. Any good horses they had were stolen either by Parliament or Royalist soldiers. So he was fed, rested and watered, to go back on the road with us on his aching back.

Raglan was an impressive place, we walked our poor broken horse over the bridge of the moat. From the top tower a voice shouted in Welsh. "Pwy sy'n mynd yno? Ffrind neu foed?"

"Ffrind." Jonathan shouted back, then he whispered to me. "Sounds like friend."

"Pa fusnes sydd gennych chi yma?" He leant over the turret wall to get a better look at us.

"Lady Howard and Colonel Jonathan Windybanks of Rupert's Foote to see

The Marquess of Worcester and his friend, the King." Jonathan's voice was getting hoarse and he wasn't even sure they understood him.

We heard the chains grind as the portcullis was wound up and the huge wooden doors opened for us.

The old Marquess of Worcester was rightly proud of his family home. It was the most beautiful place I had ever seen. The guards escorted us towards the entrance hall, our poor horse was slipping on the cobblestones. A young man wearing the Worcester livery ran up and took his reins from us, as he led him off I could see him stroking the horse's cheek and giving him an apple to bite.

I felt shabby and careworn as I stood in the magnificent entrance hall bedecked with Van Dyke paintings and bright tapestries. Flowers stood in tall blue vases, spikes of foxgloves and golden rod, making a vibrant display. The good oak furniture smelt of beeswax polish, the grand fireplace had sconces either side of it with broad white wax candles. There was an inglenook with red woven cushions, I longed to sit, but as a good guest I stood, until we were introduced to our hosts.

On the table in the centre of the room stood a stunning silver salver with oranges and lemons piled on it. I had not seen such luxury since I had left Theobalds Palace.

The old Marquess walked in with his son, Jonathan bowed and I curtseyed.

"Well, well, Lady Howard, how tired you look," he smiled, "we must get you rested and dressed in time for dinner."

"Thank you Sir." I gave a little curtsey in thanks. I could see a maid waiting to escort me to my rooms, she nodded, and I followed.

"Now, you look like a man after my own heart, a Royalist Officer, by God, I wish I was young enough to fight again."

The old man threw what he thought looked like a few good punches into the air. Both younger men smiled at each other knowingly. His son steadied his father as the effort of throwing punches had nearly knocked him off his feet.

"The King is in the garden, resting, we shall have audience shall we not?

The castle was magnificent in every way. The stairs that wound up the tower to my room were a little challenging after our long ride. I felt ridiculous having to hold the maid's hand to help me get to the top.

"His Lordship wanted you to see the view, he is very proud of his land." She opened the arched wooden door, the window was open, filling the room with light. Treetops waved and danced in the errant breeze. The maid's voice was gentle and lilting. Her welsh accent strangely comforting to me.

"What is your name?" I asked watching her pour water into a bowl so that I could wash.

"Merryn." She smiled. "Most people call me Merry." She was tall and willowy and had a fine figure, I could not stop my mouth from asking.

"Why are you not married Merryn?"

"Ah, when the war is done perhaps," she smiled, "I have a good place here. I see no reason to leave a palace where all is provided, to live in a hovel with thirteen brats."

I laughed. "Why thirteen?"

"My mother's lot." She turned to the dresser as she spoke, looking for something. "Where are your boxes Lady Howard? Did they not bring them up?"

"I have lost all. I have only what I stand up in, a half dead horse, and my companion who guards me." I took off my dirty clothes and stood in my filthy sweat stained shift.

Merryn went to a clothes press under the window and pulled out a Chinese silk dressing gown, it was bright red and green, gold dragons danced around the material breathing flames from their bewhiskered mouths.

"This was my lady's you may borrow it until I can find clothing for you." She shook it out and lay it on the bed, I had not seen anything so beautifully fashionable for a long time.

I put it over my shoulders and dropped the dirty road stained shift to the floor. As she scooped up the filthy clothes to take away to be washed I asked.

"Where is the mistress of the house? I should like to thank her for her generosity."

"She died in childbed." Merryn sighed. "The babe stuck half in half out, it was upside down, so could not breathe."

"That should not have killed her." I thought about similar cases in Oxford where we had greased the child, and although not allowed by law, made a small cut to allow a bigger exit. We had many successes where the babe lived.

"The physician came and cut the babe in two to to get it out." She shuddered. "Twas terrible to behold."

"My God, my God, the man was a butcher. How was that allowed?" I expounded as I held on to the bed post to stop myself fainting. The blood rushed in my ears. I understood now why Merryn preferred to remain unmarried.

"His Lordship asked the Doctor to save his wife. He could not, she died of the childbed fever anyway." Merryn bundled the clothes under her arm and clattered down the circular staircase. She raced off but I could see the tears streaming down her pretty face.

When I was alone, I stared out of the window at the view, the moat looked deeper from this height. Birds flew past the window into the rustling trees, the Welsh landscape tumbled away from the castle; rivers ran, cows grazed, sheep bleated. If it wasn't for the soldiers in full armour patrolling the grounds, you would not believe that the country was at war. My thoughts turned to the poor young woman whose dressing gown I was wearing. I blessed her with silent prayers.

I felt better after I had washed. By opening many doors I found the closet and poured the muddy water out of the toilet into the moat below. I was brushing my hair when Merryn came back with some clothes for me.

"The King would like to see you." She smiled. "So I have brought some of the old mistresses dresses that may fit you."

I was slightly insulted, the Marquess' wife was aged when she died. Surely clothes more fitting to the current fashion could be found for me.

Merryn read the disappointed look on my face. "I am a good seamstress madam, we can make good with these. She threw armfuls of dusty, crumpled silks and shifts onto the bed. They had not seen the light of day for many years.

"Beggars can't be choosers." I said under my breath, disappointed.

The King sat with Jonathan, the Marquess, and his son, on the lawn outside the huge door to the hall. On the table were beautiful Venetian glasses rimmed with gold. A large glass jug stood behind them, full of lemonade. Lemons and sugar, such a luxury. The men turned to watch me enter as Merryn directed me through the wooden panelled hall towards them.

They all stood up. Even the King.

"What a beauty!" The old Marquess smiled warmly, "take a seat my dear."

Merryn was as good as her word, her work was immaculate. She had torn all the old lace off a dark green silk dress and pressed it for me.

She had provided me with a white shift with Belgian lace around the collar and sleeves that I could pull through the cuffs and decollage. To that she had added a cream underskirt she had found, with a matching cream stomacher embroidered with pearls.

Everything fitted me well as the skirt tied at the back and the stomacher, although a little broad, was partially hidden by the dark green silk of the bodice. I wore my own pearls wound around my neck three times and tied with a dark green ribbon that Merryn had found for me.

She had dressed my hair by pulling most of it into a bun with my face framed with ringlets made by curling tongs. Merryn had obviously missed dressing the ladies of the household. She was wasted as a general servant.

When I was powdered and painted and dressed in the dark green silk and pearls, I looked every inch my Lady Howard of the Court of King Charles.

Jonathan smiled proudly at me, the King took my hand and led me to seat near to him.

"Dear Lady," he smiled, "what a pleasure to see you looking so well."

I sat down, a footman poured me some lemonade. I sipped it, enjoying the treat.

"We will soon be on the move, leaving this most delightful respite." Charles smiled, the dark rings around his eyes had gone, he looked better than I had seen him for a long time. "You of course must move north to Lord Dunbar."

I lowered my eyes as I spoke. "I wish to see my home again. Oxford, sire. If my daughter is alive she may have made her way there."

He smiled, "I wish to see my son and daughter also." He put a finger across his lips to stop the stutter. "I understand. However Oxford is under siege Madam, it would be dangerous."

"Perhaps we may go as we came here, as weary travellers?" Jonathan suggested.

"No." The king smiled. "For through the generosity of my dear friend here you will leave in a coach. It is a long journey to go to Lord Dunbar." The King smiled warmly at the old Marquess. "Shall we have a game of bowls before dinner?"

We left them to it. William, the son and heir showed us to the parterre. Jonathan asked to be excused to wash and change clothes if any could be found for him.

"It's so beautiful here." I watched as ducks flew over us to land in the nearby lake.

"We will lose it all for entertaining the King." William sighed. "We have chosen the deep blue sea over the Devil."

"I have met Cromwell." I wandered along through the box hedges. "He seemed cruel, single minded, and avaricious to me."

William followed me. "Most soldiers are, it's how they work. From what I hear he is the Devil indeed."

"He gave me leave that my Manor would not be ransacked because he killed my Lord Howard by mistake." I looked up at him.

"Do you believe him?" He asked watching my face.

"No, that is why I want to go and see for myself." I turned back towards the castle looking up at the magnificent turrets. "But the King refuses."

"I can send a messenger for you." He looked over the lands belonging to his family, his broad hands leaning on the wall at waist height. We could see the King bowling with the Marquess on the lawn in front of us.

"Father is letting him win," he smiled, "wily old dog!"

"I have lost everything," I turned my back so that he wouldn't see my tears.

"Not everything." He smiled as Jonathan strode towards us wearing a good pair of black breeches, a singlet over a white shirt, and clean yellow hose.

"It seems to me that you still have good friends and we will provide you with coin for your journey."

"Why?" I asked as we watched Jonathan leap the box hedges to come towards us.

"Because it will be our turn next." William's voice was sonorous. "So I will do what I can for any Royalists left standing. For myself I care not. I have already lost everything that was my life here."

"Ho," Jonathan smiled as he approached, "I have been sent to fetch you all to dinner."

Over dinner, around the great oak table dressed with exotic fruit and sugar cherubs, we discussed what we had seen and done. Jonathan was animated and tried to pick every detail from our adventures in case it was of any use to the King.

"My armies?" He had asked. Jonathan told him what he knew, where they were gathering under Rupert, Maurice and the other Commanders.

I could not keep my eyes open, it was a warm evening, I had eaten very well for the first time in many days. Dry bread and cheese had been our food, and I was grateful for it. The superb meal tonight was of swan, trout, fresh garden salat, small fruit pies with cream and small brightly coloured sweetmeats gilded with gold. Red wine flowed copiously into the gold rimmed glasses, a true luxury. I felt content, full, tired, and wanted my bed. I was leaning on my hand on the table. My elbow slipped jerking me awake.

"My dear Lady Howard, do you wish to retire?" The King smiled.

"If you please your Majesty." As I watched him, I was strangely getting the feeling that this would be the last time I would see him. I shuddered.

"Are you all right madam?" William asked looking worried.

"Someone stepped on my grave sir, that is all." I got up looking round for Merryn to help climb the turret to my bedroom.

William waved a broad hand to his footman. Soon a tall muscular man had swept me into his arms as if I weighed no more than a feather, and with Merryn in tow, he carried me up the tower stairs to my bedroom and gently put me down on the doorstep.

"Thank you, Evan, you may go now." Merryn smiled at him. He winked at her cheekily.

"You have made a conquest." I smiled unlacing my dress.

"It is of necessity," she smiled picking up my underskirt as I stepped out of it.

"When the time comes, he will look after me."

"When do you think that will be?" I asked unpinning my hair.

"Soon, my Lady, very soon." She brushed my hair over my shoulders. "Not tonight, not tomorrow. You and the King will be long gone. Far away before we face our Armageddon."

"I will pray for you." I looked up at her, worried. "I wish this war would end."

"We all do, but women have no say in it or it would be over tomorrow." She peeped round the door as she closed it. "Goodnight my lady."

"Goodnight Merryn." I climbed into the large four poster bed and was asleep in a moment.

The following morning I woke to find that I now had boxes of clothes packed. A coach and four were at our disposal, I was pleased to find that Evan was to be on the coach for our protection, and Merryn was coming with us. Jonathan had shaved, keeping his moustache and goatee beard, dressed in borrowed finery looking like the true Cavalier gentleman he had become.

The King shook our hands, I had a feeling of dread as we touched. The old Marquess and his son were not so formal, hugging me and wishing me good luck. We were to go to Cardiff, from there a ship would take us to Liverpool. Evan and Merryn were to return to Raglan after arranging for us to take a Cutter to Glasgow.

After that journey, I will never travel by ship or cutter again. The seas were rough, many people mortally sick, even the crew, which frightened me. We reached Liverpool to find we had lost two overboard, no-one had noticed until we docked, by then it was too late to find them.

The Cutter was pretty, it's fine figure sat in the harbour like the younger, prettier sister of the dark ships moored against it's wall. But travelling on it was sickening, yes it was fast, too fast for me. I was so scared I asked Jonathan to tie me to my bunk as the little boat pitched and rolled in the mountainous seas. I was sure we were going to die.

By the time we docked in Glasgow, I couldn't feel my legs, and the world was rotating around in front of me. I sat on my boxes on the quayside while Jonathan, who fared worse than I, spewed his guts into the sea.

“At least it was quick.” he said wiping his mouth on his kerchief.

“Never again.” Was all I managed to garble at him.

Our coach had arrived and we heard the coachman calling for us, his Scots accent so strong we didn't understand him and almost missed getting on board.

“Well - green -yous are.” He laughed looking at us, “Never get me on one of those.” He pointed to the cutter.

We wobbled to the coach and sat inside smelling of sea salt and vomit.

“Here we go laddie.” The coachman handed Jonathan a tankard, “Get that inside ye.” It was whiskey, Jonathan gave some to me. It burnt, but it took the sickness off and we were ready to get underway on the next stage of our journey.

A Scottish Wedding, August 30th 1645

When I first saw Kirk Castle rising tall and majestic from the lush dark forest surrounding it, my heart filled with dread. We were but a few miles inland from the coast, we had passed the ruin of Dunbar Castle once belonging to the family of the man I was to marry, slighted by the Scottish Parliament Armie over a hundred years ago. Parliament had not changed much, they seemed to slight any castle, house or home of importance, standing and beauty.

I sighed, Jonathan sitting in the coach beside me gently squeezed my hand in a comforting manner.

"Don't leave me." I pleaded urgently. "Don't leave me here alone."

He pulled me to him and held me tightly against his chest, my face powder covering his new black doublet in pale dust.

"Never my love. It breaks my heart to see you so freely given away on a whim by the King." He kissed my forehead.

I sat up, we were drawing close, I dusted the powder from my lover's black doublet with my hand. As the horses pulled the coach slowly up the incline to the castle a chill breeze blew through the open windows, not unpleasant, carrying with it the fragrance of rain freshened air and pine trees.

We could see the castle now, four square, a turret at each corner, painted with yellow stucco that made it sit uncomfortably in it's sea of green. It looked like a celebration cake. The horses found more even footing as the mud turned to gravel as we grew nearer. My heart was in my mouth. Tomorrow I was to marry Lord Dunbar, a man I had never met, on command of my King. Not to do so was treason.

I dreaded the thought of sleeping in his bed, bringing up his children, leaving my true love and my Oxfordshire life forever. I choked back tears, I had only just found Katherine and Richard again.

I had received a letter from them at Raglan. It had been sent on to various places that the King had been, hoping that I could be found nearby. I had little time to read the news from home as the King insisted we leave for Scotland almost immediately.

With little chance of returning to Oxford I was devastated. I wanted her to come to Scotland with us. I gathered from her writing that Katherine had just found out that she was with child. A journey of such magnitude was too much for her. I could not ask them to travel to my wedding through the war torn countryside.

I had wanted to deliver her baby myself, but I had to leave her in her aunt Susannah's care. I knew she would do everything she could for my darling girl. But she wasn't me, and I wasn't going to see my first grandchild born.

"We've arrived my Lady." Jonathan leant across me to open the coach door as the steps were put in place. I stepped out taking the hand of a footman waiting by the coach.

Standing waiting to greet me was a tall, thin, muscular man of about forty five.

He had auburn hair to his shoulders, burnished with bright red streaks over his ears and forehead.

He smiled broadly at me. "My Lady Howard," he beamed obviously pleased at what he saw. I felt he was looking me over as if he would a prize mare.

"May I have the honour to present myself and my family to you?" He bowed graciously.

On closer inspection I noticed the red streaks over his forehead and ears were sword cuts. "I am Lord Alec Dunbar, and these three excellent creatures are my children. Alec my eldest is nine," the little boy bowed solemnly. "Iona," he smiled at a pretty red haired little girl who bobbed a curtsey politely in front of me, "who is six." A tall dark haired girl with large eyes and a pretty mouth walked forward and begrudgingly curtseyed to me. "This is my eldest girl Anne, named for my wife."

"I am also called Anne," I smiled at the girl.

"Anne you may be, but I will never call you mother." She turned on her heel and walked sullenly back into the castle.

Lord Dunbar looked surprised. "I apologise Lady Howard on behalf of my daughter. You must be tired from your journey, please follow me." He had a slight Scots brogue much like my father. No woman wants her husband to sound like her father however pleasant his voice, I thought to myself. I looked longingly at Jonathan standing behind me, as was his place in this world.

"Your servant may go into the hall, I believe they are just about to eat." Lord Dunbar offered me his arm. I ignored him, picking up my skirts from the dusty gravel. "He is not my servant Sir." I snapped briskly, "He is Captain Jonathan Windybanks of the Oxford Armie, he is my protector, also my chaperone as I have no ladies."

"Then he will eat with us." Lord Dunbar smiled kindly as he led us to the grand dining room.

Jonathan looked around the grand panelled room, heavy tapestry curtains at the windows, fine silver plates and glasses dressed the table. Sweetmeats in the shape of sugar shepherdesses sat between the flower and fruit plates. Neatly dressed servants waited to serve us.

Lord Dunbar sat at the head of the table, I to his left, his daughter Anne to his right and Jonathan next to me. Lord Dunbar picked up a snow white napkin and placed it over his shoulder as was the custom.

Anne flashed her eyes spitefully at me, watching me drape my napkin over my shoulder as she copied the adults.

"Anne is not dining in the nursery today with the other children, it is her treat."

He smiled.

I was thinking that this rude, petulant child needs no treats, but to be punished. I suddenly remembered myself at her age, I wasn't far different in attitude, but mother made sure I was punished for any slight misdemeanour. Very early on in my life I learnt the old adage 'might as well be hung for a sheep as a lamb' using it to anger and confound my mother whenever I could.

"The war seems not to have touched you Sir." Jonathan sipped some mead poured for him by one of the manservants.

"It touched me enough five days ago at the Battle of Kilsyth. Under the Marquess of Montrose we routed William Baille sending 4,000 of his men to their Lord. We wait Sir, on tenterhooks for the Parliament of Scotland to regroup and take all we have."

"Surely not," I breathed heavily wanting to go home to Oxford before this began. "Will this war never end?"

"Only when the King is exiled and Parliament run the country." He said bitterly. "Let us talk of other things."

"Serve the soup Donald before it gets cold." A hungry young Anne snapped, looking at a young footman by the serving tureen.

What a precious child, I smiled sarcastically to myself.

"Cock-a-leekie," Alec smiled, "we hope you like it."

The soup looked thin and unappetising, but as we ate, we strangers found we liked it well enough.

Anne was staring at me. "Father had many bastards," she blurted out, "they share our nursery."

"Anne, God forgive you." Her father scolded.

I sipped my soup watching her eyes to see if she was trying to rile me. "That is good, for I am past childbearing age. It will be lovely to have a house full of laughter and playful noise." I looked across at Lord Dunbar. "How many children do you have Sir?"

Her father was scarlet from the neck up as he answered. "Please call me Alec." He looked across at Jonathan who was hiding a smile by dabbing his lips with a napkin.

"The three you have met, they were with my dear wife Anne." He coughed, "there are four others, three boys and a girl." He bridled a bit as he leant forward towards me, "all from ladies of quality, none from my pushing myself on servant girls you understand."

"God forgive you Sir, do you intend to carry on in this fashion when we are married?" I asked jokingly, pretending to be angry.

"No, no." His Scots burr became very pronounced. "Two are children of my youth by Lady Forfar, twins, we were espoused but not yet married in the eyes of God. She died in the birthing of them." He said sadly. "They are young men, seventeen now"

"I am sorry for your loss." I sipped my soup, it was getting cold, we were talking too much. I noticed how he did not ask about my life and losses.

"I like my elder brothers." Anne piped up, "for they belong with us, I hate the other two father, for they do not belong here."

"Aye, aye, ye've said enough girl – go to your room." Lord Dunbar was becoming a shade of purple that clashed with his auburn hair.

"No thank you." Anne said politely, breaking her bread to bite it.

I was coming to like her in spite of herself.

"Angus is two and Peg is three, their mother is Prince Rupert's niece, she wasn't much older than me, was she father?" Anne smiled happily, having thrown all the skeletons out of the cupboard and on to the dinner table.

"She was sixteen when she came to us, eighteen when she left." He coughed. "It was a mistake."

The servants stood waiting to serve listening to the conversation, except one young dark haired maid who was trying to stop herself giggling.

"A mistake you made twice." Anne laughed. "She was married off quickly to a minor Palatine Prince, isn't that it father?"

"Anne." Alec growled at her. "Why are you so..?"

"Truthful?" She pushed her bowl away and the servants moved into action swiftly removing bowls and spoons to put pewter plates and knives in front of us.

A haunch of venison raised on the estate, Alec said proudly, was brought in with great ceremony. One of the maids poured red wine sauce over it. A grand salat followed with a plate full of a small blackish blood pudding called Haggis.

"You must have an excellent cook." I smiled.

Lord Dunbar shifted uncomfortably in his seat as our glasses were re-filled with wine.

"Lucetta should have been my wife," he whispered to me. "She came to us on a visit with Rupert while my own dear wife Anne was still alive."

"Ah Prince Rupert," I sighed, "that well known match maker."

"Anne had been dying of a cancer of the breast for many years. I was thinking at that time she would go to God at any moment." He sighed, "but she made a good recovery, and Lucetta was married off before any more harm could be done."

"Mother was very inconvenient, she did not die for another year or so." Anne munched some salat. "Did she father?"

Lord Dunbar narrowed his eyes at his daughter. She smiled at him.

"Your wife must have seen the children." I cut myself a piece of venison, crispy on the skin the meat running juicy with fat and wine. I wiped my fingers on the napkin on my shoulder.

God knows what Jonathan was thinking of all this, he kept his counsel, listening to the conversation.

"Yes, she had met Lucetta, even given us her blessing." He sipped the wine.

Anne coughed annoyingly as if to break the flow of the story.

"She was sanguine about it."

I sat eating my venison and salat listening to Alec.

"We were supposed to be a family, Lucetta, my children and the two children she conceived here."

"It was a shame then, that mother continued to live for so long." Anne said spitefully. "I hate them, every day I see them, I see stupid Lucetta."

"Anne." Alec barked at his daughter, "I'll no tell ye again."

"So why me? Why now?" I asked watching his clear green eyes.

"Rupert told me you were a Lady in need of protection, I am a good man, and I am also in need of protection - from my children!" He frowned, narrowing his eyes at the smiling petulant Anne.

"Did he not think Sir, that as a Lady with my own Manor, that I might have had plans of my own?" I asked.

"Before Rupert left for Bristol he told me that life under Fairfax and Cromwell would be hard. He liked you well enough to offer to take you away from it." He sighed. "Can we not eat?"

After dinner Alec and I walked in the garden, it was getting chilly as we wandered together. He wanted me to see the view over the box garden to the purple mountains beyond as the sun was setting.

He offered me his arm – an old fashioned gesture – my father used to do that for my mother.

We walked through the fragrances of the herbs and flowers.

"You know Alec, that I do not love you."

He smiled, "Nor I you, but it is the King's wish."

"So it is." I said as we walked on together to the point where we could see the view across the purple hills.

"A marriage of inconvenience." He laughed and I joined in.

Twelve of the clock on the following morning found us standing in front of a Minister of the Church of Scotland, saying our vows. We had both been dressed magnificently in our finery. I wore a court dress provided by the Marquess of Worcester's dead wife. It had a silver silk underskirt and overdress of cream and gold tapestry embroidered with blood red peonies. Over which I wore the pearls that Artful had bought me years ago, which I had long believed to have been stolen from a lady of the court. On my head I wore a red felt hat dressed with heather, curled hair in the latest Oxford fashion showed around my forehead and cheeks. I held a bouquet of flowers from the garden picked by Alec's daughter Anne, she had tied it with a pretty cream ribbon.

My first wedding to my dear Lord Howard was not nearly so grand. We married in St. Giles, with just Susannah's family and a few of Howard's friends. We didn't even wear our finery.

Today, I looked the part of an aristocratic wife, even if I did not feel like one.

I smiled at Lord Dunbar as he walked to join me, dressed in gold and silver like myself. He wore breeches that matched his doublet and had changed his yellow hose to white. I was terrified he would wear a kilt like some of his clansmen, I mentioned this to his daughter Anne, she must have said something to him because he smiled at her as he walked towards me.

I felt I was watching the wedding of someone else who wasn't me. All this ceremony was happening around me, and yet my heart wasn't in it. I felt I was on the outside looking in.

After the ceremony there was the traditional race from the unmarried men of the party to grab the bride's garter from her knee. Jonathan beat all comers and stole my garter, waving it in triumph as he danced around. It was also tradition that he stole a kiss, which he did. To his credit and my relief he did not linger too long about it.

The food was sumptuous, piled high on the table waiting for the guests. I sat beside Alec, his children sitting beside him on his left, and Jonathan sitting beside me on my right. Alec's older twin boys had already taken part in the battle of Kilsyth earlier in the month. They could not stop talking about it, reliving and relishing every dramatic moment they had experienced. Laughing at their escapes. The boys were identical in looks, and for my sake one was wearing a blue ribbon on his doublet so I could learn to tell them apart.

The two children of Lucetta, sat side by side looking frightened and occasionally bursting into tears, the little girl sobbing, "Mutti, mutti."

"What are they saying?" I asked Anne, "Do you know?"

She smiled proudly at being asked a question. "It means mother in their tongue, they have only learnt a few words of Scots, but Lucetta spoke to them in German all the time. I expect they miss her."

"How long has their mother been gone?" I whispered to Anne, not wanting to upset the children more. "Not long, she came back to see them with her cousin Rupert a few weeks back."

I made up my mind there and then that the children of Lucetta should be with their mother. How I was to accomplish that I wasn't entirely sure, but I was sure my step-daughter Anne would help.

After dinner, the music struck up. Fiddles played and bagpipes roared breathlessly. I saw a late arrival join the party, covered with dust from riding hard, but still tall and handsome. Prince Rupert walked across to us both, Alec bowed and I curtseyed.

"So I find you very merry." He smiled. "I am not so."

Alec called a servant to pour wine for Rupert. They walked to a corner of the room with their glasses. They sat talking seriously, ignoring me completely. Women have no place in war apparently. Perhaps someone should tell the She Generalissima, Queen Henrietta, a more organised and better strategist than her husband. Their letters captured at Naseby were full of her advice that the King had ignored. He would rather lose armaments and men than take council from a woman.

I danced with Jonathan, siding shoulder to shoulder with him, he smiling at me. "This should be our wedding." He whispered to me as we joined hands to make a four and moved in and out in time to the music.

The music changed and one of Alec's twin sons tried to teach me to reel, but it just made me laugh, and we ended up laughing at our attempts to dance.

Lord Dunbar looked across at his son and nodded to him. It was obvious to me that while I was dancing with one of the family, Alec was making sure I could not dance with Jonathan.

It was soon time for the moment I was dreading, I had drunk much wine and mead nearly making myself sick instead of insensible. We were escorted to the best bedroom, the

Minister blessed the bed as the men stripped Alec to his shirt and the ladies stripped me to my shift. The musicians played as the party pulled at our clothes, then led the raucous singing crowd into the hallway. "Put the doggy in the pen, pen, pen," they sang, "make a mother of the hen, hen, hen." They laughed.

It was time for us to perform. Once the act had been committed we were properly man and wife, bound together for life.

I lay on my back in the bed in my shift feeling strangely lonely and cold despite the amount of mead I had drunk that evening to take the edge off.

"May I madam?" Alec asked politely pulling my shift up to my waist.

"I am your wife." I said reluctantly. I closed my eyes as he mounted me, feeling like I was being sired like a mare.

I did not want him to mark me as a whore, so I did not engage with him, I could not show experience. I did not know this man at all, I did not know how he would behave if I did.

He rolled off and lay on his back.

"The job is done." He shouted to the raucous jeering crowd outside the door. "The woman is now my wife!"

There was much cheering as the crowd made their way back to the main hall to drink Alec's wine and eat his food.

I pulled my shift straight and made for the chamberpot where I relieved myself mightily, then to the jug and bowl to wash myself with the lavender soap I had brought with me. I thought Alec was asleep, I wondered if I could get to Jonathan to bring the coach round and leave. Go home to Oxford, Katherine, Susannah and my Manor. Even as I was born a Scot, everything here was strange to me, this was not my home.

"It will get better you know," his Scots burr evident in sleepiness. "If it doesn't I promise I will let you go." He yawned. "I yearn for another also, beyond my reach, behind Heaven's gates."

"Alec, be tender to me, even if you don't love me. Can you do that?" I asked worried.

"I've done my duty, it was pleasant enough," he stared at me in the flickering candlelight. "Despite what my daughter told you, I am not one for whoring like other men." He sat up on his elbow, his long auburn hair tousled across his shoulders, watching me. "Let us see what we make of this."

The next morning we went down together to break our fast. Many of the wedding guests were at the table waiting for us. They smiled and clapped and wished us well. I was seated next to Prince Rupert.

"How do you find yourself?" He grinned. "Well satisfied I hope."

"Trapped." I looked up at him. His face fell, I could see he was angry. He could take the defeat at Bristol, but not a defeat from a woman.

"I will make the best of it, don't you worry." I took some bread and cheese. Most were eating porridge, but I did not care for it this morning. "Take your niece's bastards back to Germany with you. They cry constantly for their Mutti, they are lonely and miss her."

"They are babes, they will grow out of it." He took a drink.

"If you do not take them with you when you go, I will kill them both." I stared at him wondering if he would believe my bluff. "They are more than I can stand."

"You could not." He spluttered.

"I have many potions, remedies and poisons in my medicine chest, it would be easy." I frowned. "If you take my chest away, I can make more from the herb garden here." I threatened.

"What would I tell my niece's new husband?" He asked stunned.

"That they are your bastards and you want your niece and her husband to bring them up, for which you will pay them." I sipped my drink. "If she is any true mother, she will not want the payment."

Prince Rupert stood up angrily knocking his chair over. Everyone looked up, Alec frowned at him. He laughed it off and apologised. He turned to me, and whispered. "They are your husband's children."

"Either you take them, or I will." I held his gaze.

"God damn you woman," he hissed at me.

"He already has Sire, and you helped him." I got up and walked to the window to look at the garden. He stormed out.

Alec came to talk to me, worried Rupert had upset me.

"No, no," I smiled, "He just wants to take Lucetta's children to visit her, I told him you would not allow it."

Alec smiled, "Of course I would allow it, they cry for their mother all the time it would be good for them." He squeezed my waist. "Shall I tell him they may go for a visit?"

"Yes, please do, he is not pleased with me." I smiled stroking his arm gently.

I walked back to the table and sat down next to Alec's daughter Anne.

"Did it work?" She whispered trying to hide a smile.

"Yes it did my girl, the babes will be with the mother they miss so much, and you will be free of them." I picked up my pewter cup and sipped from it.

"Thank you." She smiled, "I knew we would get on the moment I saw you."

I liked men, always have, but until now had always been in the fortunate position to choose my own. That is why Howard and I allowed Katherine to marry for love. As it turned out it was the best thing we could have done. Richard had stood by

Katherine as his vows had stated, through sickness and health, protected her, provided for her, and loved her.

William Worcester was as good as his word, he had sent messengers to my home and that of my aunt Susannah and letters from Oxford began to arrive within five days of my arrival and marriage. Exhausted riders believing that they had messages of great import, leaped from their horses and handed the letters to my new husband who looked at the address and handed them directly over to me unopened.

It was Richard's support that led he and Katherine from Boyons' Manor to my home to live. He left his hard faced mother to fend for herself. Free of Lady Boyons' constant bullying and criticism, Katherine had started to become the joyful young woman she used to be. She was happy to be with child, even though she was scared, for she was not strong after her illness. I thought that Susannah and I could bring her through it, but thanks to Rupert I was stuck up here in the wilds of Scotland with Alec Dunbar and his many children. The letters were a comfort, but made me realise how far away I was from my true home. How I longed to be there with Carpenter moaning about his chores and my good natured maid Ruth, busying about the kitchen and garden.

I am not the first woman to be told whom to marry, and I don't think I shall be the last.

Since the wedding night Alec had stayed in his own room, Scottish Parliament forces were advancing towards us. He spent many hours discussing tactics with his Royalist Officers and his excitable twin sons who, from snatched conversations that I overheard, couldn't get out to fight and die quickly enough.

It was nearly August, the midges hung in the trees of the estate like black clouds of dust. It was warm this morning, the sun being up early. I got up to wash. I had busied myself during past weeks, writing letters trying to find places to send Alec's younger children to safety. Age was no defence against the rampaging soldiers we were expecting. We had been sending money and plate abroad to Holland where a few Royalist families we knew were living in exile. A couple that I knew from my Oxford days, the Ryders, were now in Amsterdam. Themselves Scots, they had agreed to take Iona and young Alec for the duration of the war.

My maid, Hettie, the dark haired pretty young girl who had giggled at my first dinner at Kirk Castle, came bringing a jug of warm water for me to wash. She bobbed a curtsey at me.

"What is Hettie short for?" I asked as she poured the water.

"Heather, but everyone here calls me Hettie." She folded clean linen towels and put them on the chair by the wash basin. "Mistress, can you take me with you when you leave?"

I looked surprised. "When am I to leave?"

"Tis talk, aye throughout the castle, the Parliament Army will slight the house, anyone left here will be murthered, such as happened at Basing House madam. All have places to go, my father was killed in battle and my mother died of grief, I am alone."

"Of course Hettie, if I am to take you, I will take daughter Anne as well." I looked at her puzzled. I wondered how she heard of Basing – so far South – but then she listened. She must have listened to every breakfast and dinner conversation about the war, since she served the food at both.

"When is this supposed to happen?" I asked watching her face.

"September, they are marching toward us now according to the Gillies." She looked scared. "Thank you madam, I will make you proud, I will work hard."

"You do not have to convince me Hettie, I have already agreed to take you."

As she left, the wooden arched door to my bedroom shut with a bang, caught by the wind. It made me jump.

I walked to the water, soaped a wash cloth and started to wash myself. I let my shift fall to the floor. It was a warm morning and the heather soap was pleasingly soft and bubbly. I was drying myself when Alec walked in quietly.

I quickly wrapped the white linen around my body.

Strange to say I had forgotten he was there, almost forgotten he was my husband, I hadn't seen him since the wedding night.

I could see him reflected in my mirror, smiling, bare chested, his hair free around his face. He was only wearing his uniform breeches. He padded bare footed across to me; tall, handsome, finely made, muscular and wiry. His eyes darkened as he approached me from behind. His cold hands stroked my back gently making me shiver. He traced the scars my mother had made during my childhood, so deep that they had stayed with me the whole of my life. He ran his fingers over the raised ridges caressing my skin softly.

"What is this my Lady?"

"My mother used to beat me with a switch, sometimes a carpet beater. I was a hoyting girl much like your Anne, and I was punished for it." I answered trying to pull the towel to cover the scars.

He carefully undid the towel letting it drop from my body. The marks of my mother's attentions ran down to my buttocks.

"She didn't mark me where anyone could see, so my back was constantly opened." I bit my lip, "I am sorry Sir that I am not the bride you expected."

"Ssh." He said softly as began to kiss the scars, his lips were cool and my skin was starting to tingle as his soft morning beard tickled my skin, making goose pimples down my arms and legs.

He turned me to face him kissing and caressing me. I could feel him rising hard through his breeches, he undid them and they fell to the floor. He picked me up as if I weighed nothing and threw me on the bed.

Afterwards, as we lay entwined together, he stroked my cheek. "I am I hope, a good man. I try to be. Even though, I have made many mistakes, but I do not think accepting you from the King was one of them."

I smiled at him. "What makes you think that?"

"Kirk has never run so smoothly, everyone seems happier you are here. Even Anne!" He smiled broadly. "Despite the death threats to my children!"

"Rupert?" I asked.

"He told me all that passed between you, but Anne told me that you were distraught that such young children should be separated from their mother. As it turns out they will not be safe here. So you have done a good thing." He held me to his chest, close for the first time. I saw the sword scars across it.

"I would not have hurt the babes..." I watched his face.

"I know. Anne told me it was an empty threat to make Rupert act."

"What did you say to him?" I asked sitting up.

He smiled. "Och Lassie, I told him he should not have set me up with a mad woman at the King's command, and that he must take the babes for their own safety." He laughed. "Such a long journey with two mewling infants who never seem to stop crying, I'm sure he will enjoy it."

"One defeat after another." I laughed.

Alec smiled at me. "If you carry on like this madam, I will be in mortal danger of falling in love with you."

Do not, I thought to myself, do not. I am going home to Oxford and my family. Do not complicate matters.

Jonathan was pacing about impatiently in the garden, light rain had started to fall, he took shelter under a great oak to keep out of it.

I raced towards him pulling the hood of my cloak up.

"Why are you so late?" He asked frantically. "Are you all right my love?"

My face flushed red, "Yes, yes. What news?"

"Parliament are almost upon us, we must leave today if we are to survive," Jonathan said breathlessly.

I pulled him towards me and kissed him passionately, which puzzled him.

"Then we must go, get the coach ready, I have already packed everything I need to take, we will be taking my maid Hettie and little Anne with us."

"Why? They will slow us down." Jonathan looked at the purple mountain in the distance.

"Because they have no-where else to go. Alec and his boys and the men here will fight and take their chances, but you and I both know what will happen to two pretty little girls in the midst of war."

"What will your husband think?" Jonathan asked. His thoughts were running wild overtaking his good sense. "We were to be married were we not? Now I have been cuckolded twice before I am even your husband."

More than that I thought to myself, but I could not be so honest to a man already in pain. "Later my love, if all goes well we will have the rest of our lives together. God bless us and preserve us all." I took a breath and we ran back towards the castle in the rain. "Alec said on our wedding night, if I hated it here he would let me go." We stood in the doorway and I shook the rain off my cloak. "But everything has changed." I thought of his kind smile and gentle touch. I did not hate him. I was homesick, hating being so far away from my home and family in Oxford.

"In what way?" Jonathan asked, "Do you wish to stay?"

"No, no, my love. He says he will help us to leave, so we must go. Have you muskets loaded and dry powder?" I asked worried. "The coachman knows the way?"

"He suggests for speed that we go by sea part of the way."

"No, I will not do that. It is by the road only, I will pay him extra for his trouble."

"When can we go?" Jonathan asked. "Shall I draw the coach around while the drawbridge is still down?

"Yes my dear, I will go and tell Alec, then bring Anne and Hettie and my boxes to the door."

News had travelled fast. Inside the castle boards were being put up at the windows and those not boarded had musketeers in them ready to fire. I felt as if I was sitting on a powder keg about to blow.

As I crossed into the long hall, pictures and hangings were hurriedly being removed and loaded onto carts. Plate was being hidden in secret cupboards behind the oak panelling. I knew that was no good. I had seen how in Oxfordshire, Lady Boyon's furniture and floors had been hacked to pieces in the search for hidden silver. When she returned to her manor, the house was a burnt out shell.

"Anne," Alec rushed across to me, "you have heard? They are closer than we thought."

"I know, I had Jonathan keep watch for us. Let me take Hettie and Anne with me." I hugged him. "Husband keep safe, if it is your home or yourself, save yourself."

"I have nothing to save myself for." He said looking over my shoulder at Jonathan. "I will fight to the last dear Anne for my home. Worry ye not, I have many heirs, there will always be a Dunbar at Kirk." He kissed me. "Now go."

His daughter Anne, ran up to kiss and hug her father.

"Goodbye Mischief." He smiled at her. "Try and be good till I see you next."

Anne burst into tears as Hettie hurried her into the coach. We had four outriders with us, all armed with muskets and swords. Pistols and a sword were left inside the coach for us to use if need be. Musket balls in little bags were stacked on the floor, near to a box of black powder.

"Away, Away." Jonathan shouted to the coachman. He could see a cloud of dust rising on the brow of the hill as the Roundhead's cavalry approached.

"Don't look back," he shouted to us, "keep your heads inside the coach."

The horses flew at breakneck speed across the drawbridge, the coach lunged dangerously to one side on two wheels, I pushed the girls to the opposite side of the coach so we would remain upright. It fell straight with a loud bang. I could hear the creak and rattle of Kirk Castle drawbridge chains as the door was shut, and the loud bang of it's portcullis as it fell to protect the door.

We could hear the crack of musket fire, we hoped we were just out of range.

The girls were screaming with fear so I grabbed both of them and held them tightly to me. "Save your breath, save your energy, we may yet have to run for our lives."

Fettiplace Manor, Oxford 1675, aged 80

I sit in the top Gallery of the house, overlooking the gardens. Medlars, peaches, apples and pears grow in abundance against the soft cream stone walls. I sit in the good light by the window, pen in hand, all my adventures done. I am missing being young. Sometimes I feel I have never been young. Held a man in my arms, or bore a babe from my body. It all seems so very long ago now. I have white hair which I hate, pains from the rheumaticks that I treat myself and put up with, and I write.

I write my life for no one would believe it if I told it as a story. But I hope that some time in the future long to come, people will know of me, my loves, my hurts.

I go by Lady Howard still, even though the Protectorate didn't recognise me. I have lost my Manor, my home. This was despite the framed parchment on the wall signed by Cromwell's own hand, saying we were not to be touched.

The house was razed to the ground, all my good household stuff taken, my books burnt, my servants shot against the stable wall. I shuddered to think of it. My brave Irishman Gardener, who tried to protect my young maid Ruth from rape, but had his head stoved in by club muskets.

The cows and sheep were driven away to feed Cromwell's New Model Army. My furniture burnt to cook them on. So many years past, yet as I write, I am there again anew. The heartbreak now, is as fierce as it was then.

We lived for many years in Bear Meadow in poverty with my aunt, relying on the kindness of friends. From having everything found for us to having nothing at all.

Richard's mother did not lose all. She did lose Richard to me. It didn't bother Lady Boyons overmuch. She was inventive to say the least, she managed to stay the hand of the avaricious Puritans by marrying one of them. He was a portly red faced Colonel. She then became Mistress Springate and lived again at her old home, Boyons Manor under it's new name, Armesgate Manor, laughing, telling anyone who asked that it meant bone-yard.

Kindnesses to me were repaid by my making salves, tinctures and medicines. Which I mixed to ease the hot, cold or phlegmatic humours of my patients. Sometimes with the help of Susannah and Alec's Anne we birthed children. Susannah's family had been wiped out by the plague when Fairfax took back Oxford, the black death marched in with the soldiers in their camps, taking her husband and two teenage children with it when it left.

I thought the plague was God's punishment for the damage the Puritans had wrought in the town, for they endured the worst of it. The wealthier parts of Oxford such as St Aldates seemed to suffer the most under Puritan destruction. Many beautiful churches were desecrated, their statues pulled down as idolatry. Soon afterwards the plague burned throughout the Parliamentarian camp, nothing seemed to abate it. They prayed to the God that they had looted, raped, and destroyed for. He didn't listen, plague pits were opened up around the outside of the town. Some so full, that arms and legs poked out of the earth in a grotesque salute to say goodbye to the world.

Still, throughout all of this, the town's tradespeople and the university's gowns were as separate as ever. Fights broke out now and then as they always had, this time however, the combatants were brutally rewarded by the Commonwealth soldier's swords, as they were reminded to keep the peace.

We had to attend Church every Sunday or be fined. Susannah, Anne Jonathan and I walked together, heads down, not talking. We had heard that two women who chatted on the way to church were thought to be enjoying themselves. Not thinking of Sunday as a Holy Day. Their punishment was to be pilloried. Humiliating and painful. Everyone had enemies, everyone had grudges. So we kept to ourselves and our household.

As I think back over my life, perhaps I might have fallen in love with Alec if there had been no Jonathan or no war. I could have lived back in the land where I was born, in Kirk Castle high on the hill a few miles from the sea.

Alec and I were only a few years apart in age, both of us had no expectations of the other. In the short six weeks I had lived as his wife, I had found him to be kind and thoughtful to me and his children. Particularly little Anne who was his favourite. She looked so much like the woman he had loved so dearly. His wife Anne had many portraits around the castle, the one in the great hall showed a dark haired beauty with stunning grey eyes and a warm generous mouth. She had the fashionable oval shaped face so favourited by the Cavaliers, prettily framed with curls.

The last portrait made of her was in Alec's private apartments. She is wearing a dark blue silk court dress with slashed sleeves showing a white shift embroidered with gold underneath. Around her neck a long string of pearls draped loosely, pinned to her stomacher on the right hand side with a gold brooch inset with diamonds. Her hand protectively over the growing babe in her body. The babe who would not be born, but was part the spreading cancer that eventually consumed her.

They were all together now, Alec, his twin boys, and his much loved Anne. Buried in their desecrated kirk in his slighted castle. Kindness, youth and beauty buried together in their home by Parliament soldiers. Alec and his sons fought fiercely and bravely together. The Roundheads in awe of their strength afforded them the privileges of their rank and allowed them to be buried with their kinsmen.

His precious daughter Anne came with me to Oxford and we lived in quiet harmony in Susannah's humble home. We were a strange little family, Jonathan and I, Susannah and Anne, and her two maids who had grown up, married and were now young widows. They had both returned to Susannah's house, the only real home they had ever known. They still washed the sheets by trampling them, but there was little laughter these days.

Anne was constantly talking in her fading Scots accent of going home to see her father and her brothers when the war was over. Not knowing, for I hadn't told her, of the letter I had received soon after we arrived in Oxford. The one with Cromwell's seal. The one that told me of his death, of his sequestered lands. There was no point in telling this bright young girl happily living in our household that her home was destroyed and her family with it.

There would be time enough for that.

In those days we were all poverty stricken, gone were the days of good provender, we lost weight, we went hungry. The God fearing Puritans had emptied our stores and our purses, so there was no money for travel. I asked young Anne, how could we travel as far as Scotland? Two women on our own? The roads had become dangerous with Highwaymen, so we told Anne she had to wait. She would stamp her foot and slam the doors and tell us that she hated us, but when the storm had passed, she would come and say she was sorry and that she would wait for better times.

On the days when we had hardly any money for food I often wondered if my plate and precious household silver were still hanging from the strong rope inside the chimney of my Manor, crumbling away in the lush green countryside. Although I had heard they had all been shot, I still held out hope that some of Ruth's family escaped.

I am very tired, my eyes hurt. I wear little wire framed spectacles which helps ease them. Writing ever writing for fear my memories would be lost, that I would not count. That my adventures were a tapestry that would fade and turn to dust before they could be known.

I stand and look out of the window, holding on to my writing table for I am frail now. I have outlived two husbands, my lover and my daughter.

I have been lucky enough to meet with my King's son Charles II, The Merry Monarch, and be at his coronation. I shared my memories of his father with him, how he played bowls calmly at Raglan while plotting to re-take his Kingdom. How he never paid his debts, Charles, his son, decided to try and pay as many as possible. It was not possible. He had inherited the near empty coffers of the Protectorate, so the debts remained unpaid.

I told him of his father's bravery on the day he died at Whitehall, dressed in his finery and wearing his garter star. How he kissed his children before he left them, a scene so moving that even his captors cried. To Elizabeth he held her hand and kissed her, and bade her not to cry, to his son Henry he clasped him to his breast telling him "Do not let them make you King."

The crowd were shocked, silent after it happened, a couple of women fainted.

Many people rushed forward with kerchiefs to collect King Charles' blood as it dripped through the scaffold, for it was well known the King's blood had healing properties.

"Behold the head of a Traitor!" The executioner had shouted.

"Judas!" a man shouted from the crowd. A general cheer went up, I still cannot fathom why. No one seemed particularly happy, not even Cromwell's wife, who was watching, hiding behind a curtain in a coach nearby.

I feel a bit shaky today, I hold on to the window sill and ease my bones onto the cold pale Hornton stone window seat to sit so I can look out.

I have lived to yet another Summer.

The sun is bright on the lush green grass of the garden, I watch my great grandchildren run and jump over the box hedges. It is a fine game. My daughter Katherine bore Richard a daughter and a son. She died birthing the son, the loss of blood was so great, neither Susannah with her great experience or myself could stop it.

Richard didn't marry again, even though he was a widower at twenty-five. We brought up the children, he, I, and Susannah, as best we could.

It is my beautiful daughter's grandchildren that I watch at play now. Her daughter was named Anne for me, although I disputed it at the time, feeling I had been unlucky. I did not want to pass a name with a curse attached to it to a pretty child. She married a Puritan boy called Providence, handsome, with big brown eyes. We hated him on first sight, but he bought our respect, with his care of Anne, his family were merchants of the new 'middling class', he was a clothier and sold good stuff to make clothes.

The son that caused my daughter's death by being born a ten pound child to a slight frail girl, was called Anthony. After St Anthony, the patron of lost souls. He married a Fettiplace girl, a silly empty-headed fair beauty, and it is through his marriage that I sit in the tower of their house with food on the table, watching their children play. He works as a doctor, trained in Oxford like his great uncle Thomas. I have time for Anthony, he treats me as if I were still a woman of fifty, we discuss cures, new and old, herbs and treatments, salves and medicines. He sees me, not my age.

Memories of the Protectorate

1653 – 1659

I write what comes to mind and it is not always in the order you suspect. I have called this chapter memories of the protectorate, but I cannot stop thinking about my poor little King Charles.

Oliver Cromwell swung to and fro with Charles' fate, losing Lord Fairfax in the process. One moment he was for saving the King and controlling him through Parliament, the next he wanted his head. It rather depended to whom he was speaking. How this rough hewn farmer came to have so much power is beyond me. When I asked Richard, he joked it was because he had killed everyone else.

The Lord General, Black Tom Fairfax, his friend and battlefield commander walked away after the death of the King. He prayed for the King's soul during the execution. He was accused of wearing the 'Kings Colours' because he did not sign Charles' death warrant, all the time pleading mercy for him. Black Tom thought he knew his brother in arms Cromwell too well. Not well enough it seems, for when Thomas Fairfax's daughter married the Duke of Buckingham's son, the boy was imprisoned at the Tower, and Black Tom had to argue with The Lord Protector for his son in law's freedom.

So many awful events. I have to say, I am glad the Lord Protector suffered at the end. He had murdered so many Englishmen, even leaving his own injured men to die in the burning ruins of the once magnificent Basing House, so as not to slow his progress down. The talented Dr John Bastwick who had helped my Katherine at Naseby, was called to London to help Cromwell. The Lord Protector was beyond help, suffering as he was with malaria and a stone. It was a hot summer the year he died, and die he did. We heard rumours here in Oxford, that poor Dr Bastwick was accused of turning Royalist and poisoning him.

From what Katherine told me of him, Dr Bastwick was a kind man, he was deeply interested in the human condition, if Cromwell did die under his care, it was not for lack of his attention. It may be, and I only say this as a midwife who has ended more than a few mal-formed creatures lives; that he may have been kind enough to give the Lord Protector a medicine to ease the pain and release his soul, when there was no further hope but suffering. It was more than he deserved.

How my mind jumps about, age, I suppose.

It was a cold, dark, Christmas eve in1654. It was the first Christmas after Katherine's death. Under the Protectorate, Christmas had been banned, it suited our little family we had been in no mood to celebrate. Susannah was putting the babies to bed. I was sitting in front of the fire trying to keep warm by rubbing my hands in front of the dying flames. Richard was reading a broadsheet that he had paid a penny for by Oxford Castle gates.

A penny we could not afford by the way, but it was Christmas still for us, and he loved to read the latest news.

“My Lord.” Richard expounded. “This is bad news indeed.”

“What is the trouble?” I asked getting up from the settle.

"The woman who helped cure Katherine's leg, Goodwyfe Vasey, has been stoned and burnt as a witch. Matthew Hopkins says she had been in league with the Devil." His face reddened with fury, I had never seen Richard so angry. "My arse she's a witch."

"I know Mistress Vasey, she gave Jonathan and I a room for the night when we were hard set to in Leicester." I said poking the fire trying to get some heat out of it. Jonathan came in carrying logs and heard the tail end of the conversation. "Is that not so my love?" I asked.

Jonathan and Richard stared at each other, as if they had only just met for the first time.

"Were you the stable lad in Leicester?" Asked Jonathan. "We had not met then."

"We are now made all so much older by the war, but I see you now sir! By God, to think we were all in the same house at the same time." Richard smiled as realisation dawned. "I wish we had known then."

Mistress Vasey was a Goodwyfe and well known for her remedies; dark haired, tall, efficient, astute with money. She was precise in her dress, dark and Puritan like. Her younger sister, the baker's wife was completely different; round, ruddy and full of fun. What they missed in sisterly likenesses, they made up for in kindness and generosity. Their mother had taught them to 'be not inhospitable to strangers least they be Angels in disguise.' Their mother used bible quotes to teach her children, as she herself had been taught.

The bible was the last thing on Felicity Vasey's mind as she hung naked by her wrists from a beam in her dairy. Her long dark hair had been loosened from it's tightly wound bun and hung over her shoulders covering her breasts.

"She looks like a witch does she not?" The young thuggish ignorant face of the self-styled Witchfinder General, Matthew Hopkins, walked around Felicity, admiring the sight of this naked tethered woman, who in her thirties still had a fine figure and long legs.

"Shave her." He ordered brusquely. "So we may better see the marks the Devil himself has made on her."

Matthew Hopkins paid some women of the town to become prickers for him. For a few pence they would mark with a pin any deformity, wart, or mole on the alabaster body of Felicity Vasey. An elderly woman approached with a razor and shaved the hair from Felicity's armpits.

"Mistress Herrick." Felicity's voice trembled, "Did I not cure you of your rheumaticks?"

Mistress Herrick avoided her gaze, thinking of the coins chinking in her apron pocket. She could eat tonight.

Felicity looked across to the younger woman who was about to shave her private parts. "Edie Carpenter, I birthed your babes did I not, and cured them of the croup?"

Edie ducked her head and got on with the job in hand. "Didn't get my husband to stay tho' did 'ee?" She said spitefully hacking away at Felicity's pubic hair.

"You didn't ask me." Felicity flinched as the razor nicked her skin.

"So you could have done that eh?" Matthew Hopkins flicked Felicity's long dark hair from her breasts with his riding crop to admire them. Then he put both his hands on her paps to fondle them. "Just checking for marks madam, be still." He smiled spitefully, squeezing her nipples so hard it brought tears to her eyes. Felicity looked up at him, her voice like acid. "Of course not, look at her." She shot a look at Edie. "She's a slattern – what man would want to live with that for the rest of his life?"

Edie, looked up shocked.

Felicity stared at her, "What mean you by helping this foul creature? Easy coins in the hand mayhap?"

"Careful ladies, for the devil speaks through this mouth." He put his filthy, dirty fingers into Felicity's mouth and she bit him hard. She wriggled and kicked in the air frantically, catching Hopkin's fellow witch hunter John Stearne between the legs causing him to collapse in a heap.

"Tis proof enough to me." Matthew grinned lasciviously at the writhing naked woman. "Cut her down."

Outside Felicity's well ordered home, a crowd was gathering, spreading rumours about her, each one worst than the last. How she had cursed a child so it had grown up an idiot, how she had stopped the water to the town during the occupation so that only her well did not run dry. How she put a spell on the cows and sheep so that they died before they got to market. How she always had money in her purse and food on her table when they had none. The noise of the rabble was getting louder as Felicity was dragged outside into the street as naked as the day she was born. A few decent men looked away, but many of the rougher sort whistled through their teeth in appreciation, cat calling of what they should like to do to her.

May Miller, Felicity's sister was in the Bakery with her seventeen year old son holding one arm and her forty year old husband holding the other.

"I must go to her." She screamed through her tears. "She needs me, she's my sister and she's done nothing wrong." She struggled from their grip. "Please Dusty, let me go, please." She pleaded.

"They will kill you too, and burn the shop down. It will finish us all." Her worried husband put his arms around her. "May, I beg you."

"Not if I do it properly," she screamed. "We have a plan, do you not think that Felicity thought that one day this might happen?"

The men stared at each other as May explained what she was to do.

"Mother," the boy watched her frantic expression with disbelief, "will it work?"

"It has to." May said going to the store cupboard and taking out a small bottle of green liquid given to her by Felicity a few weeks earlier. She grabbed a lamprey from a barrel of water in the larder. "I am ready, come with me or stand back, I will take what comes."

Both men grabbed a doublet, put it on and hared down the few hundred yards to Felicity's house, where she was being tormented.

"Ah sister." May said as nastily as possible. "So, found out at last are we?"

Felicity looked up and smiled.

"She's the sister, get her." Shouted someone from the crowd.

"Keep away from me you crow's arse. May the Devil take you sister." Felicity's mouth twisted horribly as she shouted over the crowd.

May came up to her sisters face. "So it is true then?" She spat.

"What do you here?" Asked John Stearne still clutching his wounded crotch.

"Come to see justice at last." May laughed. "I have brought you a present sister." May took the Lamprey from her apron, it wriggled and squirmed towards Felicity's face. She tried to turn away from the wriggling black eel with it's mouth full of sharp teeth.

Felicity screamed, as she opened her mouth, May poured the green liquid into her as the distracted crowd watched the lamprey try to escape into Felicity's throat. May took the Lamprey, broke it's back and threw it into the street. Felicity smiled. "Thank you my dear sister." She whispered almost silently, before it looked like she had fainted in shock.

"Press her, press her, kill the witch." The enthusiastic crowd had paid Matthew Hopkins well for this entertainment and they wanted to see it completed. May, Dusty and her son went into Felicity's well ordered and tidy house, picked up the few chairs that had been knocked over in the struggle to get her out, locked all the doors and pulled the shutters closed on all the windows.

May stood on the front door step and shouted as loud as she could above the rabble. "Alls of you who knows me, knows this was my family home, and my family home it will stay, Dusty has a musket at the ready and any of yous who tries to take it off me after I have waited so long for it, will be shot."

A cheer went up from the crowd, May and Dusty were the same as them, they were good bakers, good townspeople, worked hard and gave credit tabs, the crowd thought they deserved a bit of luck.

Felicity's body was placed on the cobblestones in front of her house, a large wooden door was placed on her white marble like body. There was not a mark on her, a few people noticed but kept quiet, having a loose tongue when the Witch Finder General was in town was not a good idea.

Stones were placed on the door, more and more, heavier and heavier, there was a loud crack as Felicity's ribs broke under the weight and breath expelled from her lungs in a loud gush. Blood trickled from her mouth and her body.

May sobbed heartily in Dusty's arms. "Thank God she didn't have to suffer that."

"The poison worked very quickly didn't it mother?" Her son handed her a brandy from her sister's cupboard. She pushed it away.

"As soon as it touched her throat she was gone." May cried. "My poor sister. God forgive me."

"Why the lamprey mother?" He asked sitting beside her, watching his father pace towards the window then turn back.

"Twas a silly game we used to play as young girls to scare our mother witless." She wiped flour from her apron onto her face as she cried. "Scared her stupid it did, we would put them in our mouths and pretend they had jumped in. We bit them in our front teeth so they couldn't wriggle forward. Eels are eels they will hide in any dark place given the chance. Then we would run into the garden, take them out and dance about and laugh at her. Did us no harm, apart from today, when I hid the bottle of poison behind the lamprey that everyone thought I was torturing her with." May said with her voice breaking as if to cry.

"We should pray," Dusty came away from the window. "For Felicity's soul, so good as it was, and for us, that we may not live to see that bastard Matthew Hopkins or his like ever again."

The family knelt together hands clasped and templed towards Heaven and prayed for forgiveness for all.

Richard put the broadsheet on the table beside him. "The back is blank mother, you may use it to write on if you wish."

Paper and ink were luxuries. Even in Oxford at that time.

I picked it up and read it through, getting ever more melancholic at the news it held. Lord Fairfax had been made a Doctor of Civil Law in Oxford. A skirmish led by Cromwell in Burford had stopped a Cavalier uprising. I sighed, I could read no more without further upset, so I folded the paper to make four small pages and cut it apart with my sewing scissors that lived tied to my apron with a ribbon. I placed them on the writing table by the window.

We could hear Susannah's footsteps on the wooden stairs from the bedrooms, it had taken an age but both children were now asleep. She didn't tell me at the time, but I learnt later that if cradling and warm milk didn't settle them, then a tiny drop of laudanum added to their bottle did.

The sun moved lazy shadows across the lawns, lengthening them. The garden is getting cooler and the children have been called in by their nurse for their evening meal. Their pretty, vacuous mother Letitia would be in her bedroom primping herself ready to go down to dinner with her husband and his relatives. Letitia actually didn't object to us living here, she is constantly match-making for Alec's daughter Anne, and I earn my keep by teaching her children to read and write, which being illiterate herself, she appreciates.

As they run into the house for their supper, I move to my great chair, my luxury, the one with the soft goose feather cushions. My mind is roaming through my life again, I have heard it said that before you die that your life will flash before your eyes. On the battlefield perhaps, but in a country house on the outskirts of Oxford, it moves as slowly as I permit it. The King wanted me for a spy. A spy? He had better, more articulate, more adventurous women than me to do that work for him. I did help Artful in a matter of the King once. I helped him dress the stocky Prince James as a young woman after he had escaped from the Tower of London. We contrived to get the petulant youth on board a ship leaving for Holland. It was managed by getting him into a dull brown fustian frock and bribery with a meat pie. Teenage boys are always eating! Artful escorted him to the Netherlands and I stayed at home. Hardly the adventure to get your heart beating with excitement.

Anything of interest that I heard that might be of use was forwarded to the King by a letter signed in cypher. Your friend in the Cause. There wasn't much, as my own life was so pell mell, rushing towards event after event.

I rest my head back on my feather pillows. Life has come full circle, I have enough luxuries now, and enough company to make it bearable. All these memories are making me tired and I'm frightened to go to sleep. I don't want to die. I want to fall asleep and wake up as a young woman on a coach coming to Oxford. I want to start all over again, and do it properly this time.

The light through the window is fading, it must be time to light the candles, I try to get up but cannot move. In the last of the sunlight I see a figure by the window. It's Jonathan, he is wearing his finery. He holds out his hand to me.

"Shall we take a walk in the garden my love?" He asks.

"I am too tired." I smile at him.

"Lean on my arm my darling girl." His smile lights up the room. "A little walk in the garden together, and then we can rest."

I get up, more easily than I have of late, feeling lighter, happier, and take his arm, we walk together through the window.

Somewhere in the hollow rooms of Fettiplace House I can hear crying, it sounds like Anne and Anthony. I do not understand why.

Glossary of Terms

17th century words with their meanings

Almanac	weather predictions, household and farming advice for the year ahead
Apothecary	pharmacist, chemist
Baldrick	a belt to hold a sword and scabbard – see scabbard
Back & breast	armour for the back and chest
Black dog	depression
Black Lion	venereal disease
Black powder	gunpowder
Black-work	stitching; black embroidery on white linen (berries, leaves etc)
Bear Meadows	now known as Jericho
Blued/blacked	armour protected from rain and rust by applying heat and oil by a blacksmith
Bodice/Bodies	type of corset laced front or back sometimes in two pieces

Brazier	metal container to hold a fire
Bucket boots	thigh length leather boots used for riding, tops turn down when not on a horse
Buff coat	yellow suede cavalry coat to be worn under armour
Bum roll	stuffed crescent shaped linen roll worn tied around the waist over the shift but under the dress to make the bottom bigger
Buss	a kiss
Closet	a secret room off a bedroom
Clubmen	local farmworkers who band together to protect their homes with clubs, usually too old to join the army
Club musket	using the shoulder piece of the musket as a weapon
Codpiece	a patch of material tied between the legs of men's breeches that could be removed to allow urination.
Coif	a linen cap worn by women to cover their hair
Courses	periods, menstruation
Cow pox rash	a red rash that milkmaids got on their hands from milking the cows, later found to protect from other illnesses
Cunny	labia
Dog Cart	a small two wheeled cart used for shopping or carrying children
Dogge	nickname for a man's penis

Dorset Buttons	intricate hand made buttons for expensive clothing
Doublet	a jacket with two arms
Dutch Coat	a cloak that can be made into a jacket with arms
Farthingale	a bell like frame made of cane and linen to be worn under skirts to make them stand out
Finery	court clothes, banqueting wear, the best clothing you have
Flints & stones	firelighter
Frog purse	fashionable item, example in Ashmolean Museum, Oxford
French style	kissing open mouthed
Fundament	anus
Fustian	a dark hard wearing rough cloth
Garde Loo	look out! – bastardised from French regardez vous
Gillyflower	vagina
Gob	mouth
Gobbets	a piece of food just large enough to fit in your mouth
Gruel	a thin soup or porridge
Honiton	town in Devon famous for it's lacemaking
Italian style	homosexuality
Jakes	toilets

Journeyman	horse and cart driver delivering goods round the country
Kerchief	a piece of linen used as a scarf around the neck
Lamprey	a common jawless river eel used for food
Laudanum	drug used for pain relief and to induce sleep
Lavender water	used as an antiseptic
Maid	virgin
Maidenhead	virginity
Melancholic	depressive
Medlars	a sour green fruit smaller than an apple best eaten rotten
Mite	smallest amount of money possible
Montero	a peaked woollen soldiers hat that pulls over the ears like a balaclava
Morpheus	God of sleep
Paps	a woman's breasts
Pell mell	rushed, disorderly manner
Pennyroyal	an abortive herb
Physics	medicines
Pilgrim badge	proof of going on a pilgrimage to see saints relics
Piss	urine
Piss pots	pewter or china pots to urinate into

Plague	black death or bubonic plague
Plaister	a mixture of medicines in a powder which solidifies when spread on a wound.
Posset	a warm drink containing alcohol, cream, herbs or fruit juice. Each household had it's own recipe.
Pox	smallpox
Press	a large wooden box to store clothes
Pricking	marking spots, warts, moles on the skin with a pin
Protectorate	the time after the Civil War when Cromwell and Parliament ran the country
Provender	food and drink
Quickening	feeling a tightening of the womb after conception
Quicksilver	mercury
Restoration	restoring Charles II to the throne after the Protectorate
Rue	an abortive herb
Salt	used as an antiseptic
Salt Petre	potassium nitrate
Salve	cream for treating wounds
Sash	a long piece of coloured material worn from shoulder to waist or around the waist to denote rank and authority.

Scabbard	a leather sheaf that holds a sword onto a baldrick
Shift	full length linen petticoat with sleeves
Singlet	jacket without sleeves, like a waistcoat
Snapsack	a large bag with shoulder strap, closed by buckle or button
Small beer	a weak beer sometimes mixed with lemon juice
Stone	kidney stone
Tace	be quiet, an order
Tallow	animal fat used to make candles
Tankard	a pint mug made from pewter or leather (blackjack)
Tansy	yellow herb for food colouring
Tincture	a small amount of medicine dissolved in alcohol
Wet nurse	a recent mother employed to breast feed a child that is not her own

Printed in Poland
by Amazon Fulfillment
Poland Sp. z o.o., Wrocław

51844418R00132